JANE AND THE WHALES

Caitlin Press Inc.
8100 Alderwood Road,
Halfmoon Bay, BC V0N 1Y1
www.caitlin-press.com

Edited by Helen Guri and Anna Nobile.
Text and cover design by Vici Johnstone.
Cover image by Sandy Tweed.
Printed in Canada

Caitlin Press Inc. acknowledges financial support from the Government of
Canada through the Canada Book Fund and the Canada Council for the Arts,
and from the Province of British Columbia through the British Columbia Arts
Council and the Book Publisher's Tax Credit.

Canada Council   Conseil des Arts   BRITISH COLUMBIA
for the Arts   du Canada   ARTS COUNCIL

Library and Archives Canada Cataloguing in Publication
Routley, Andrea, 1980-, author
        Jane and the whales / Andrea Routley.
Short stories.
ISBN 978-1-927575-23-9 (pbk.)
        I. Title.
PS8635.O875J36 2013   C813'.6   C2013-905493-6

JANE AND
THE WHALES

Stories

Andrea Routley

CAITLIN PRESS

Contents

Habitat

It wasn't the mess that concerned Ray about the garbage outside, but the fox. It had started coming around, dragging away oily paper bags, Styrofoam take-out boxes, and throw-away crusts of stale bread that collected along the row of plastic garbage cans. Ray had first spotted it in spring, when the lawn was still flooded in places by melted snow. He rushed outside in sockfeet, clapping his hands and shouting, "Go on, save yourself!" He couldn't stand to see a wild thing living like a transient. The fox trotted away, but returned as Ray reached the porch. "At least eat something decent," he said, and went inside to retrieve some wieners. When he came back, the fox had already started up the trail by the clay cliffs that rose up at the end of the cul-de-sac.

Ray knew he should get out of bed and deal with the mess outside. His daughter, Lana, was over for her visit and he didn't want her to think he didn't take care of the place. She used to come every weekend, but it had become more sporadic as she got older. Now, at fifteen, he was lucky to see her twice a month. A year ago, when he was in Edmonton for his sister Colleen's funeral, he picked up a ginger-haired guinea pig from a pet store. He thought a little pet would help Lana feel more like this was her home, too.

She raised her eyebrows at first, made some crack about being too old for a guinea pig. "I think my class had something like this in grade two," she said.

"How can you resist this cute little face?" countered Ray. He'd already named her Bubble Gum. Lana said it was a good name, "in an ironic kind of way," whatever that meant. Still, Ray hoped he could change her mind about the place, that she might live here more permanently for a while.

A magpie rapped outside, alerting others to the stray garbage. For now, he would let them have their fill. No damage in that. They were town birds through and through, and there was something about their noisy squawks that seemed a fair punishment for human mess. *We're the greediest creatures on the planet*, Ray thought, and resolved to defrost some caribou for the fox. He took a drag of his hand-rolled cigarette, watching the smoke slither up to the grey ceiling. The venetian blinds were closed and a navy blue wool blanket hung over them, so that only dim, pixelated light made it into his room. He tapped the ash onto the glass-topped nightstand beside his bed, a relic from the eighties. *This is how fires start*, he thought. *Some dumb shit passing out in bed with a cigarette in his hand.* He thought of his daughter in the room beside his, and butted the cigarette in a pile of wax where a candle used to be.

Ray usually slept on the couch, but he didn't want the place to feel like a flophouse while Lana was here. It wasn't easy to fall asleep in his room; it was stuffy. No surprise, considering he hadn't vacuumed in a year, but Ray managed to ignore the carpet. He was home on "stress leave," they called it, so he no longer had the sterility of the wildlife management office to measure his own cleanliness against. He hated being in the office anyway. The older Ray got, the more indoor his job became. He used to work in the bush, not that he ever liked shooting wolves, but later was stationed at a desk, coordinating reports and recommendations or responding to e-memos or searching for some online data or other. His fingers mashed clumsily on the keyboard and the monitor glare hurt his eyes, already reliant on thick lenses.

He got up and went out to the porch to watch the ground squirrels. There was a colony of them at the end of the cul-de-sac, an elaborate construction of underground tunnels. Lana was outside putting a box on the curb.

"Bend at the knees!" Ray called. And she bent at the knees. He watched her label the box, F-R-E-E, with a black marker. Ray lit another smoke and sat on the top step of the porch.

"Can I have a smoke?" Lana said, passing him.

"No." Ray was surprised. "It's a nasty habit. I need to quit but it's been forty-five years—"

"I was just kidding," she said, and went inside.

"Lana," he called, "That's not a box of perfectly good stuff, is it?"

"It's free!" she called back. Ray got up to inspect. There was a lamp, a clock radio, a picture frame, a red *New Testament*, a paperback entitled *Caring for Your Guinea Pig* with a picture of two children petting a brown one, and a curling iron.

The screen door squeaked. "That stuff is free, Dad."

"This?" Ray held up the clock radio. "Is it broken?"

Lana slouched. "No, it's not broken, but I just use my cell phone for my alarm. There's too much stuff in my room. It's like a rat's nest in there."

"It's going to *get* broken. You can't put a free box out around here. The punks in this neighbourhood will just make a mess of it. The little shits across the street—they're all over the place, like an infestation. Do you know, Lana," he said, using the clock radio as a pointer, "what their ringleader did to my lawn chair?"

"I don't know, Dad. I'm sorry. I'll just leave it out at home, okay?"

"Dismembered it, that's what."

"Then I'll take it home and leave it out there."

Ray dropped his arm. That was the real problem, Ray knew. Lana wouldn't call this rundown duplex home if she was too good for a perfectly functioning clock radio.

Lana picked up the box. "Can I keep it in the living room until I leave? You want to put that back in?"

"But it works?"

Lana nodded. Ray gave up and placed the clock radio in the box, but its new position was precarious, so he moved the guinea pig book and settled the radio in deeper. He was about to replace the book when he stopped.

"Did you read this?" he asked.

"I think so." Lana turned and headed back inside. Ray would have to do something nice now before he asked Lana to live here full time. He thought about the caribou in the freezer. Potatoes, sweet potatoes, carrots, maybe asparagus, a light beer—no, not beer, he'd hear about that from her mother. Juice. Orange juice? Too much orange. What about blueberry pie? Will she eat pie? Young women are so worried about their figures, but Lana has never said anything. Would she say anything to her old Dad, anyway? Colleen never thought much about squeezing into the latest fashions, either, if that's what it's all about. She had those chubby muffin-top cheeks all her life. Yes to blueberry pie. It's the thought that counts.

"Will you be getting hungry soon?" Ray asked her, back inside.

"Maybe in a couple hours," Lana said. "I'm going to clean and stuff."

Ray returned to his porch step. Sometimes his porch time would intersect with the girl next door. She lived there with a roommate who was never home because he worked in the bush, and her dog, a German shepherd named Billy. Ray liked Billy a lot, but recently the dog had figured out how to kill ground squirrels. After months of lame attempts, tail sky high and his nose buried in clay tunnels, his reflexes made a sudden improvement and *snap*, he'd caught one, chomped twice, and then left the poor squirrel to the little shits in the neighbourhood. Ray tossed the squirrel into the trees by the cliffs, but they probably found it eventually and dismembered it, too. Maybe not a bad thing, if you considered the food chain. At least the ravens would be able to get at the meat. They can't eat the meat if it's not ripped up somehow; their bills can't break skin. Maybe he should tell Lana about that. She might be interested in a detail like that. She was always an animal lover. When Lana was four, she went through an admittedly annoying cat-phase.

"Where are your pajama pants?" her mother would ask.

"Meow?" an upward intonation.

"Pajama pants, Lana, put them on."

"Meow!" Her hands curled like little paws in front of her face.

"That's enough, Lana."

"Meeoow—" a drawn out intonation, a passive aggressive protest. Then her mother hooked her under the armpits.

"Meow!" Quick, sandpaper tone.

And threw her on the bed and slammed the door. "Go to bed!"

Ray had more patience. He passed through phases of finding it cute, to being concerned about his daughter's intelligence, to finding it cute, to admiring her commitment to the role.

She should be an actor, he thought. "Lana," he called through the screen door, "Do you like movies?"

"What?"

Ray took a bigger breath. "What kind of movies do you like these days?"

"Why? Do you want me to rent a DVD? I'm going out for coffee, so I can," she called. "After coffee, though."

"Oh," Ray said. She had other plans. "I was just thinking, do you remember when you were always pretending to be a cat? When you wouldn't answer your mother except with meowing? That drove her crazy, but God it sure was cute. Do you remember that?"

"No. I have to turn on the vacuum, so I won't be able to hear you."

Ray looked at the guinea pig book. "Caring for your Guinea Pig," he said out loud. "I'll bet Bubble Gum doesn't like the sound of that vacuum." He opened the book to a page with the heading, *Eat Your Veggies!* There was a cartoon of a child frowning in front of a plate of carrots and broccoli, while a guinea pig sat beside him happily eating a lettuce leaf. *These herbivores require a lot of vitamin C, so be sure to give them lots of greens such as kale, collards, and romaine lettuce.* The first sentence shocked him. Ray had never seen Lana give Bubble Gum any greens. He felt a sudden outpouring of sadness and sympathy for Bubble Gum. He thought of the day he picked her out. He was still in a daze after Colleen's funeral, but, on an impulse, had turned into Pet Planet on the way out of the city. He wandered through the aisles of dog food, chew toys, grooming tools, past chattering aviaries, and the wall of aquariums. When he and Colleen were kids, they weren't allowed pets, so they "rescued" a beetle, instead, and kept it in an aquarium. They'd found the beetle in the field behind the apartment building. It was ruddy orange and black, and walked steadily through yellow grass, past empties and around assorted plastics. It walked with so much purpose.

But Ray wanted Lana to have a real pet. He had stopped at the guinea pigs. Bubble Gum was the short-haired ginger one that stayed in the corner while the rest of them scurried away from Ray's hand like they were magnetically repelled. Bubble Gum might have just been too fearful to move, or she was new. Perhaps she hadn't en-dured the hundreds of clumsy children's hands that probably pawed at them day after day. So Ray cupped her gently as if he was bending to drink, and examined her tiny face. He wanted to nuzzle his nose into her fur and cuddle her right there, but there were people. In-stead, he just said, "I'll take this one." Now Bubble Gum had been here for a year, and it pained Ray that a basic need for vitamin C had been neglected. He continued to read. *Everyone loves treats! And your guinea pig is no different. Treat your pet to melon or apple— but be sure to remove the seeds, which are toxic.* To think Bubble Gum had never received a treat. Ray couldn't remember ever giving her any fruit.

The vacuum turned off. "Lana," he called. "Have you ever given Bubble Gum any apple?"

"Apple? I think so."

Ray flipped the pages by bending the book and letting them flit out from his thumb. He stopped on a page with a cartoon hotel. *Make Room at the Inn*, he read. *They might be small, but guinea pigs* love lots of room to play! *Guinea pigs with homes in larger cages are more likely to be active—just like you, they love to scurry and hurry and hide! Remember also to give your pig lots of yummy hay, which it loves for nesting and snacking. Don't use sawdust, pine or cedar chips, or fabrics that may cause health problems, like trouble breathing.* Ray marked the page by folding over the corner and closed the book. It was no wonder Bubble Gum was always in her cave, the avocado-green colander with the door cut into it. She had nowhere else to go. For a year she had only to run from the colander on one side of the cage, to the food pellets and sipper tube on the other. The guy at the pet store never mentioned any of this stuff and Ray could remember woodchips in the guinea pig cage there, too. That's what they sold for rodents. He wondered if Bubble Gum was asthmatic, if that was another reason she didn't run around much. *Trouble breathing.* Or if her teeth hurt, if it was like a baby teething, cranky and teary for respite, but without the speech to ask.

"*Toooweeet! Tooooweeet! Tooooweeet!*" There she went. The only language she had, tooweets and whistles. Maybe she was saying, "My teeth! My teeth!" Or, "My muscles are atrophying!"

The door squeaked open and Lana trotted down the porch steps, throwing a hemp purse over one shoulder.

"See you in an hour or so, Dad."

"Lana, wait—"

She turned around and leaned into one hip. She had on a white T-shirt, brown surf shorts, pink flip flops. She stretched her toes up and down in her flip flops, revealing the black bottoms of her feet.

"Didn't you have a shower?" Ray asked.

"Is that what you wanted?"

"No. I've been—" Ray held up the book. "I've been thinking about Bubble Gum. Do you still love her?"

"Do I love Bubble Gum? Dad! That is the weirdest question."

"She needs hay. I had no idea. Did you know that, Lana? Does Bubble Gum have asthma?"

13

"Okay, Dad." Lana raised her fingers, which were clasped onto the purse strap in a wave. "I'll pick up some hay on the way home." She turned and started down the path.

Ray stood up and twisted the book into a tube. He was going to shout after her, "I do not appreciate sarcasm!" or, "I will not tolerate that attitude," but she wasn't a bad kid. She rounded onto the sidewalk and didn't look back or wave, just twisted tiny plastic earphones in and flipped along. Ray sat sipping his beer until it was empty, thinking about Bubble Gum. He had to admit, he hadn't paid much attention to her for a long time. He took care of her, provided for her, burned urine-stained wood chips in the fireplace, but was that love? And what was he teaching Lana about love if he can forget about Bubble Gum, too? Colleen would never have been so neglectful. She'd had a cat there at the end, left him with a neighbour in the building, with instructions on how much ointment the tabby needed for his eye, how much food, how he liked to be patted. She said she was going on holidays, but never returned, so the neighbour thought she'd abandoned the cat. It was weeks before her car was found. But Ray was used to not hearing from her much. It was a three-day drive just to visit and flights were expensive.

The fox was by the clay cliffs now, weaving between wild rose and sage. This time, Ray acted quickly to grab the frozen caribou. There was no time to defrost it or cut off a piece. He would have to give it the whole thing. Back outside, the fox was by the plastic bins, licking what was probably hoisin sauce off the pavement. There was no one on the street watching, no one to give him a hard time about feeding wildlife. Meat or no meat, the fox was coming around for the garbage. The least Ray could do was give it something nourishing. Ray clicked his tongue and the fox looked up, darted a little behind the bin, and then resumed licking. He knew he wouldn't be able to get close to the fox, and he didn't want to frighten it, so he threw the frozen meat across the road. It landed in the claydust trail at the end of the cul-de-sac.

"Go get it!" he said. The fox continued licking. "That's good stuff, you know." The hoisin sauce was sugary, even for Ray's taste, and he couldn't stand the thought of it causing the fox's teeth to rot, making it impossible for it to chew, leading to starvation. "Get outta here!" Ray shouted, and thumped down the walkway, toward the fox. The fox ran away, unaware of the frozen meat. Hoping he'd find it eventually, Ray went inside.

Lana's room was reorganized. She'd only taken that one box out to the road but her room looked emptier than Ray thought it should. Perhaps she'd been moving out piece by piece, like a mouse stealing chunks of bread until the loaf is gone. Her dresser was no longer cluttered with jewelry boxes, wallet-sized photos, and plastic trolls. All that was left was a scented candle. Maybe this was a symptom of growing up, the need to purge the room of childhood artifacts. But his sister had never thrown anything away. She collected dairy crates, instead, and stacked them to make shelves. Later on, she labelled the shelves with paper signs tied on with yarn: "Horses," "Stuffed Animals," "Books I Don't Like," or "Collectables," which were rocks, dead moths, bleach-white clam shells from their one trip to the ocean, and a bowl of moose droppings. "It's good to have souvenirs," she'd said.

Bubble Gum was in her usual spot under the colander. He took a food pellet and held it outside the cave door, clicking his tongue. "Come on, Bubble Gum. Let's have a look at you."

Bubble Gum didn't move. He made kissing sounds, instead, moving the pellet closer, but she remained still. On the floating shelf to the right of the window were a few teen novels about vampires and, beside them, a black seal stuffy. Maybe Bubble Gum would end up on this shelf one day. He knew it could happen. Like the beetle. He and Colleen had followed it for maybe ten minutes, keeping their distance so they wouldn't influence its course, until Ray picked it up. They took turns holding it on its back while its legs wriggled and clicked. They collected twigs and leaves, and used a plastic bag that was caught in the yellow grass to fill with sand and dirt. At home they used an empty aquarium where a goldfish used to be before it floated to the top of the opaque, green water. They made a habitat for the beetle, and put it in Ray's room. The leaves wilted, the grass went untouched. The beetle covered itself in sand. They used a twig to wake it up, get it to move, put fresh grass in with it, then flower petals, then whole dandelion heads, but the beetle didn't eat any of it. It moved less and less until one day it had simply dried out. And now it was Bubble Gum's turn. She'd get quieter, come out of the cave less and less and next thing you knew, she'd be in the closet, or a "free" box. She'd be discovered by one of the territorial male squirrels and then that would be the end of her. Maybe the fox would run off with the rest of her, get scared away by a passing car, and then Bubble Gum would be perfect raven food—torn-up roadkill. The neighbourhood brats would scare off the ravens and rip the rest of her up, throw pieces into the woods or lay guts on the swing set, then take their sick curiosity somewhere else. And that would be the end of Bubble Gum. Lana would ask what happened to her, shrug her shoulders and then go out for coffee or something. Maybe she'd say, "Poor Bubble Gum," but that would be the end of her. What would Colleen say about that? She'd say, "How could you let this happen again? How could you let this happen when all the signs were there?"

Ray took the colander away and tossed it on the bed. He scooped Bubble Gum up and held her against his chest, but she crawled up to his shoulder, nudging her nose under his ear, and tickling him. Ray laughed. "Aren't you cute!" He held her in front of him to speak eye-to-eye. "Look at those nails. You could use a trim." He placed her gently by Lana's pillows, the colander next to her. "I'm sorry to alarm you, but think of this as the camper van you're staying in while I build the cabin."

He lifted the cage off the table to the floor underneath. After a trip to the kitchen to find scissors and duct tape, he snipped the chicken wire away from one side of the cage so that Bubble Gum would no longer be confined. He stuck a few layers of tape over the wires that poked out, for safety. He found the vacuum behind the recliner in the living room and sucked up the urine-stained wood chips and feces. He tore up some of his old newspapers to replace the chips. He'd been meaning to clip the important stories and recycle the rest, but this was just as good. "It's not going to waste," he said, and thought of Colleen. Her car was found off the side of a logging road, the note on the front seat. How could he have known that the walls were too close, too high, and there was no one to reach in?

Now Bubble Gum has a home under the table, and a carpeted world to explore. He returned the colander to the cage, but left Bubble Gum where she was on the bed, half swallowed up by pillows, only her bottom visible.

When Lana returned, Ray was on the porch again, smoking and sipping another beer. Lana held up a DVD and walked up the steps with her head bowed.

"I offer this DVD, to be placed upon the altar that is the TV cupboard."

"*Twilight*? Isn't that a book?"

"I'm impressed, Dad! It's also a movie. Vampires. It's good." Lana went inside. After a moment she held the screen door open onto the porch again. "What did you do to my room?"

"I renovated it."

"I almost sat on Bubble Gum."

Ray took a drag. "Don't move, Lana. There's a ground squirrel there eating the dandelion and I think he might just come up to the first step if we stay still."

Lana stomped out onto the porch, slamming the door behind her. The squirrel ran off, disappearing into a tunnel in the grass.

"Why would you do that, Lana?"

"I spent the whole morning trying to clean, Dad. And you can't vacuum wood chips. Now the vacuum is probably plugged, and my room—"

"You're not here too much anyway, I thought. And you're just going to get busier with your friends, and then college, you know. I think it's pretty cool. No 'pretty cool, Dad'? Huh?"

"It's pretty mean."

"You know what's mean, Lana? Treating Bubble Gum the way you do, ignoring her like that. You can't just put her on a shelf and wait for her to die."

"I don't want Bubble Gum to die."

"Do you know what happens when you just forget about something? Things become unliveable. They get swallowed. You're lucky you haven't seen that, but I'm pushing sixty, Lana, and you should be happy that Bubble Gum's got some room to grow in."

"That is not what's happening, Dad. I just cleaned up in here and now it's a disaster again!"

"Praise be to you, Lana, who took a box of perfectly good stuff and dumped it."

Lana slammed the door again, shouting back at Ray, "I'm not allowed to clean *my* room? I'm not allowed to get rid of some of *my* old stuff?"

Ray's head felt constricted, as if he'd been wearing a tensor bandage. "That is a guest room!" he shouted through the screen door. "You breeze in here whenever you feel like it, chuck whatever you want," then, falsetto, he added, "'Oh, I gotta go for coffee, Dad, I gotta see my friends, Dad, it's been like twelve hours!'" Colleen wasn't like that. When she was Lana's age, she preferred to stay in and read a book.

Across the street, a woman sitting on her stoop was smiling. She'd been watching and listening, probably getting a kick out of the drama. Maybe there was nothing on TV right now. Ray felt ashamed and went inside.

He knocked on Lana's door. "Are you getting hungry now? I've got some caribou I was going to cook up."

"I don't want anything."

"I've got some sweet potatoes, too."

Lana didn't respond. Ray turned around and looked at the place. Piles of old newspapers formed short columns in one corner of the living room. Three pilled fleece jackets collected on the couch like deflated cats, and the lower cushions stuck out too far so the upper cushions fell behind. The top of the TV had a layer of dust, except for the rectangle where the broken DVD remote had been until Ray finally replaced it yesterday, before Lana came. The kitchen was just as bad: a stack of magazines on the table, a shoebox of irrelevant receipts, shoelaces and old magnets on top of the fridge, four empty planters on the counter, a reminder of the herb garden he would never get around to, and a broken ski pole leaning in the corner beside the broom. He thought of the place where they'd found the beetle, where wild grass grew, strewn with sheets of plywood, perfect hiding spots for snakes, Colleen had said. They'd called it a field, but later realized it was an empty lot. Flowers were weeds, and the lake an abandoned quarry. After it died, Colleen found the beetle in a book; found out it was really called a burying beetle and needed carrion to live, and dead mice to lay its eggs in. Found out about field mice, too, that they'd been around since the time tyrannosaurs thumped across the continent and the first ancestors of mice and humans appeared, humans evolving one way, bipedal and shoes on, and mice pursuing life with their bellies to the ground and the tops of flowers towering above. Now they were called pests.

Ray stared into the empty freezer until he remembered the caribou meat was across the street. Maybe the fox had found it by now. He should check. If it was still there, he could just rinse it off. He could boil it, make a stew. That would kill the bacteria. But there were only four potatoes in the bin, two of them wrinkled and soft, and no other vegetables. The counter was cluttered, and he didn't know what was clean and what was dirty. He heard Lana open her door, so he pretended to be busy cooking. Maybe she would like pizza.

"Lana?" he called. "What about ordering a pizza?" He walked into the living room but Lana wasn't there. The door to his room was open.

"Lana, stay out of there—"

Lana was standing beside his bed, holding Bubble Gum swathed in a T-shirt like a child. Ray was horrified. His room smelled like bad breath, cigarettes, and fermenting fruit. Except for a narrow pathway to the bed, the floor was covered with boxes of photo albums, journals, and cassette tapes. There were three garbage bags of Colleen's clothes that had never made it to the Salvation Army, a canoe paddle Ray had won at a fundraiser, and a folded beach umbrella from the summer they spent at Cobble Lake leaned into one corner. A family photo of Ray, Lana, and her mother hung above his bed. It dated from the year they lived in the cabin, when Lana was still in diapers, and her mother's hair was long, tied back with two slim braids. Colleen's *National Geographic* magazines bordered one wall like a yellow curb. There was an old TV in a wooden cabinet, a VCR and an equalizer on top, and sitting on top of that was an empty aquarium, cracked on one side.

Lana was staring at the VCR. "They don't make those anymore," Ray offered. "This won't make a good habitat for Bubble Gum, if that's what you're thinking. Your room is the best one for her."

Lana cradled Bubble Gum on her shoulder, walked silently past Ray and sat on the couch. "How about pizza tonight?" he asked again, closing the door to his room.

"I can't live here."

Ray felt trapped. He wanted to get the caribou. If only he'd bought some potatoes and pie, had a nice meal to offer her. "We can order lasagna—"

"I don't want lasagna, Dad!" She held Bubble Gum against her cheek. One of Lana's curls fell across Bubble Gum's head.

"You know," Ray said, "you and Bubble Gum have very simi-lar colouring."

"Are you—" Lana's voice broke in a sob. "Are you *okay*, Dad?"

"Honey—" Ray squeezed his lips together and held his breath. His chest tightened.

"Because I want you to be okay, you know. I really want you to be okay."

A magpie rapped outside. "Everything's fine, Lana. You don't have to worry about me." With two fingers, Lana patted Bubble Gum, who nudged her way further into the crook of Lana's neck, almost disappearing. "She sure loves you," Ray said. Lana gave an-other sob.

More magpies rapped, and Ray looked at the window. It was so bright outside, all he could see was a white square, and the dim walls of the duplex around it. A moment passed, and he could make out the magpies collecting on top of the garbage can. "I better make sure that lid is on tight."

The magpies flew off as Ray approached, landing at the top of a pine across the street. Not far from there, three ravens picked at the softening caribou, tearing off pieces, flying away to stash them under rocks or between exposed roots, before returning for more. They cache their food. A lot of animals do. Ray hoped the fox would find enough to eat. He imagined it snapping up a ground squirrel or a mouse, weaving through the spruce along the river before dashing across the highway, up the pine slopes, and into the hills where its den would be.

The Gone Batty Interpretation

Three months ago, Carol's daughter Olivia, twenty-four, took her own life. Carol tries to think of this as something written down, a mute fact about something far away. But at night, everything is close. Carol talks to her, tries to hear responses in the branches rattling against the upstairs windows.

Tomorrow, when Carol goes back to work at the Nature Centre, she will add forty kilometres to her trip to use the other bridge.

She puts the kettle on for chamomile tea and ibuprofen. She told Olivia ibuprofen was bad for her blood pressure. "I'm not an old lady," Olivia said. The skin at her temples had blue veins visible, as if the skin was less opaque there, more like a soft film pulled taut over a delicate skull. "Just sore."

Olivia was usually tired after a tour, all those nights singing in coffee shops, pubs, theatres, but this had lasted months. A loss of appetite followed by an ulcer. Trips to the doctor followed by ones to the pharmacy, just like when she was a teenager.

"There are no environmental factors I can point to," the psychiatrist had said back then. Clinically depressed, he said.

Prescribed antidepressants, and Olivia evened out. There was no more heaving tears into her pillow, one hand on the back of her head as if trying to console herself. Instead, she watched TV with Carol, sometimes staring off and absently picking a thread on the couch, but almost her old self. Carol could stop checking on her so much, opening her bedroom door a crack and whispering to the dark, "Honey? May I come in?" She heard Olivia singing in her room one night, strumming softly on the guitar. A couple of years went by, and she played at a café near the waterfront. Carol walked around with a jar, collecting donations and telling people she had no idea where her daughter got all this talent. Olivia became a performer.

Carol wonders if she was too happy about that.

She takes a couple of ibuprofen with her tea. It helps her sleep in this house. Outside, the empty pool is just a crater on the moon, the Sea of Tranquility. One summer, there was a bat in there. From the upstairs window, it looked like a black dish rag floating around, but it was fluttering on water smooth as glass, so she wondered if there was something trapped underneath. But it was a little brown bat, swimming toward the side of the pool, trying to climb up but unable to get a hold on the tile surface. Carol called Olivia to have a look, kneeled at the side of the pool.

"Can I touch him?" Olivia said.

"I don't think that's a good idea."

Olivia frowned. "I think he wants out."

"Me, too." Carol scooped it up with a shovel, and then put on leather gloves to cup the bat gently, and place it on top of the shed to sun itself.

She wasn't sure how it ended up in the pool in the first place. Maybe that bat had only wanted a drink of water, or dipped too close to catch its prey—could bats trip? How long had it been there, paddling against a tile wall? But it was nothing to worry about. There hasn't been another bat in there since. It's hard to believe that was nearly twenty years ago.

Carol takes her tea into Olivia's room, where she's been sleeping. It doesn't seem so long ago now, that first time, when Olivia was still a teenager. Carol had returned home after the movies, and checked in on her. "You sleeping?" she said, her own voice dampened by pillows, curtains, carpet, and a warm stuffy smell, tangy like fermenting oranges, but milky. Olivia needs to clean this room, she thought. She turned on the lamp. Vomit on the walls, watery and shiny where it dried like egg whites, streaked across sheets and Olivia on the carpet, sleeping, not sleeping, unconscious.

She wonders about the antidepressants, because they don't give those to teenagers any more. They say it increases the likelihood of suicide. She wants to blame it all on drugs, as if proving the cause could provide a cure for the effect.

Three days in the hospital: charcoal, appointments, new prescription. "Whatever doesn't kill you," Olivia said. This is serious, Olivia. "I'm sorry." Later, she told Carol she hadn't meant to take so many pills, that she was really going to try to get better. And then she did. She looked so happy sometimes.

She hasn't vacuumed Olivia's room, or washed the mug by her night table. A moth flutters out as she pushes her hands into the dresses and coats hanging in the closet. Carol tries to snap the moth with one hand, but it flutters up to the light, resting on the inside of the glass cover like a black spot. Carol closes her eyes. For a moment, she can almost hear her breathing.

~

A pair of middle-aged women examines the skulls in the Touch Table— beaver, crow, coyote—then moves to the case of nests. One points to the nest of moss and lichen knitted together like a gauzy sock.

"Is this for a hummingbird?"

"No," Carol replies. "Bushtit." She sneaks away because it's almost three o'clock, and she must gather up the bean bags and visual aids for the bat presentation, first of the season. She drops the bean bags, along with the laminated bat pictures, into a plastic bin. Her slim hands might have looked elegant, but they bruise so easily these days, sometimes purple from burst blood vessels. She takes the elastic out of her dark hair, untangles it a little with her fingers, and ties it back again into a droopy low ponytail. She used to French braid it for work. Olivia said her long hair made her look like an aging hippie. "I am an aging hippie," Carol had laughed.

They won't see any bats during the day, but Carol likes to give this talk because they've put up a bat box in the park, a plywood home, painted black, for the little brown bats to roost in during the day. It's not far from the lake in the centre of the park, mounted on the top of a tall post, a little ways from the trees so it gets the sun all day. It's visible from the trail, so Carol wants to inform the public, because the bat populations are in jeopardy, like everything that matters, and the white nose fungus will inevitably make its way westward, wipe out even more bats than it has already. She usually saves this last bit for the end of the presentation. Every presentation ends on a conservation note. This is mandated by the Centre—to raise public appreciation and awareness of Nature, and to promote its conservation.

Carol counts the people by the picnic table on the grassy lawn behind the Centre. This is the meeting spot for the "Gone Batty!" interpretation. There are five children, maybe aged six to ten. There are three adults. One woman has a tri-wheeled stroller with recyclable grocery bags spilling out the rear compartment. Inside, there is a sleeping toddler, lips puckered and head lolling to one side, a plush turtle tucked beside him. Looks like a Western Painted Turtle, a stripe of red down its neck.

"Somebody's tired!" Carol says.

The woman smiles. "Wore himself out at the water park." She has a sloping nose and tiny chin, delicate features which seem at odds with her ruddy, porous skin. She looks too young to be a grandmother, and too old to have a toddler. But Carol never presumes to know anything about anyone anymore. Carol focuses on the little fingers resting on his navy corduroys.

"He climbed that boat ladder thing at the park about a million times," the woman says.

"Well, he's adorable," Carol says, then introduces herself to the group. The kids sit cross-legged on the lawn, squinting in the sun. Another adult stands behind with his arms folded, legs apart. He looks like a bouncer, ready for damage control. The third adult sits on the picnic table bench, moves her long black braid in front of one shoulder, then tickles the shoulder of the pigtailed child in a red jumper. She looks too young to be a mother, but she could be a nanny.

"Does anyone know where bats live?" Carol asks. Hands dart up like the heads of geese on guard. She points to the boy sitting in front of the man, a tall kid with sharp features and narrow eyes.

"Caves?" he says.

"Yes, they do like to live in caves, but also old mines, and even attics." Carol tells the group about echolocation, how the little brown bats locate, catch, and swallow an insect every three seconds. How they probably use their sight when flying distances, how echo-location only works for things that are closer. She tells them the smallest bat is the size of a penny. It's called the bumblebee bat and it lives in Thailand. Where is Thailand? It is far away, in Asia.

"Pad thai, Conner," the man says to the boy. "The peanut noodles you like."

"The little brown bat, our most common species around here, and one that is in every province of Canada, would feel the same in your hand as seven loonies," Carol says, revealing the change in her palm.

Kids take turns holding the loonies. Some close their eyes as if imagining it is actually a little brown bat in their hands. It's not really like that, though. A living bat would feel lighter than dead weight. The child with black pigtails, a girl about six, places the loonies, one at a time, in Carol's hand.

"Thank you," Carol says. The child doesn't say anything, just smiles shyly and returns to her spot on the grass.

"So what are bats?" Carol asks. She wants to get through this part quickly, and get to the echolocation game, "Bat and Moth," before the younger ones lose interest. "Are they fish?" she prompts.

The kids say no together, the pigtailed girl looking at her nanny, as if seeking permission to laugh at this grown-up.

"Are they ... birds?"

No, again.

"Are they flying mice?"

Only two kids say no this time, and the man says, "Huh," and appears to genuinely consider this question. It was an unfair question, really, shifting from class to order.

"Bats are mammals," Carol explains, "which means they have fur and feed their babies milk just like your moms did for you." Some of the older children shift uncomfortably at this idea. "Bats are Chiroptera, which means winged hand." If they fall into the water, the brown bat turns its long webbed fingers into a raft and kicks its tiny feet to reach the shore.

The man holds one hand up. "So they're mammals, but what are they—rodents?"

"They're bats," Carol says.

"But—what are bats?"

"Bats are their own order of mammals. A quarter of all mammals are bats, and more than a third are rodents."

Many of the children's faces knot up in the centre, some saying "Eww!" The way they scrunch their faces looks like the Persian trident bat, its nose like a carnation, fleshy petals encircling the central point, the source of sound. Most children think bat noses are quite repulsive—some look like giant pig noses with nostrils bigger than their eyes, while others are like leaves pointing up to their foreheads, directing the ultrasounds. Some have a probiscus that points up and out, twice the length of their head, pink and covered in fine hairs like the stems of cold weather flowers.

"Can I kiss him?" Olivia had asked as the bat climbed up the roof of the shed.

Carol holds up the picture of the bat in flight, backlit by some photographer's spotlight so its arms and fingers can be seen in the membranous wings. Look at these pictures of bats, Carol says. Look at the bats, look. Some children touch the photos, run their fingers along the skeleton, tactile knowing.

The bats were in the shed that year. There must have been a hundred, huddled together, covering an entire wall and spilling across one corner. "I think our bat is a girl," Carol told her. So many bats must be a maternal roost.

27

"But are they related to rodents?" the man asks.

"In terms of evolution, you mean?" Carol collects the laminated pictures.

"Sure, I guess so."

She wipes the loose hairs sticking to her forehead. "Some scientists think bats have more in common with primates—the fruit-eating bats at least. But there's just not a lot known about bat evolution. The earliest fossils we have are fully formed bats, so we really don't know."

Carol feels strange saying we. It implies a collegial relationship, and she is just a naturalist. She took some courses in evolution at university way back when, over thirty years ago now. It was all natural selection back then, a world of animals stuck on the same track, stomping past each other to stay out front, some falling off with weak ankles, or collapsing from dehydration, while others, blessed with stronger bones and more fine-tuned excretion systems, continue onward. Every beautiful thing is an adaptation, something to find food faster, sleep deeper, attract a mate, procreate, pass the genes down, downward, time moves downward. It's all so mechanical.

"Can anyone tell me how echolocation works?" Carol says. The sharp-featured boy, Conner, raises his hand. Carol nods at him.

"It's like when dolphins make sounds that they can find their way under water."

"Right," Carol says. "It's a way of using sound to find things. Insect-eating bats use echolocation to find the insects." To demonstrate, Carol turns to the side, her profile to the kids, takes her clipboard and holds it in front of her, at arm's length, places her hands loosely over her eyes, fingers splayed. "Bat," she says. Pretends to think about this. "Sounds pretty far away." Then she moves the clipboard so it is only an inch from her mouth. "Bat," she says again. "Sounds pretty close!" Then she pretends to eat the clipboard, licking her lips after and rubbing her belly. The pigtailed girl giggles, but the older kids like Conner just laugh awkwardly, unsure of whether they are too old to find this funny.

"Who wants to try?" Carol asks. The pigtailed girl raises her hand, then stands and closes her eyes.

Carol holds the clipboard a metre away. "Tell us when it's close enough to eat," she says.

"Bat," the girl whispers softly. Carol moves it closer. "Bat," she says again. "Bat." When the clipboard is just a few inches away, the little girl simply opens her eyes, smiling, and sits down. She looks like a happy child, but not in the way that every parent simply wants to believe—some children cannot be described that way. Some are fussy, some are chronically unsatisfied from the moment they come out crying. Some have permanent scowls on their faces, as if they are carrying around an injustice from a past life. Not Olivia. In the corner of the shed, one of the little brown bats manoeuvred herself in that deceptively awkward way, walking on her elbows, the bat version of a seal out of water. She turned her head, her rounded ears and tiny nose, shiny eyes, and yawned. Olivia gasped as she did this, lacing her hands together. Prayed to keep them safe.

One child rests her cheeks in her hands, and then rips at the grass in front of her. Is Conner yawning? Is she losing them?

Now it is time to play "Bat and Moth." Carol explains the game as she places little blue bean bags around the lawn, marking a circular enclosure. "This is the boundary," she says. "You are all insects and this is where you live. Does anyone know what kind of insects little brown bats like best?"

"You already told us moths," Conner says.

"Good! You're paying attention," Carol teases. "I am going to be the bat. Some of you will be moths, and some of you will be shrubs rustling in the wind. You have to imagine it is nighttime, so it's very dark." The shrubs will stand in one place, whispering *sh, sh, sh*, making the sound of wind blowing off the water, eddying through the bulrushes and grasses into the oaks, snowberry and black hawthorn. Carol will close her eyes and call, "Bat." The moths will respond, "Moth." Bat, Moth, Bat, Moth, their locations obscured by the wind, but not enough to lose them.

"Like Marco Polo," Conner says.

"Yes," Carol says. Marco. "And when you're caught and eaten up, you need to stand outside the circle. Do you think I'll be able to catch one of you every three seconds, like the little brown bat?"

"Gonna be tough!" the man offers, then holds up his cellphone, ready to document his child's good time.

Carol closes her eyes halfway. A dog's leash jingles at the collar on the gravel path just beyond the picnic table.

"Your eyes are still open!" Conner says.

"Well, bats aren't blind, remember?" Carol says.

Conner looks at the man, then back to Carol, skeptical. "But then it's too easy," he complains.

Carol knows it is nighttime in this game, and moths are too small to catch with sight. She is supposed to close her eyes. She is supposed to use the "Bat Mask," a night mask with a black construction paper wing stapled to each side. The other children look equally disappointed with Carol's open eyes. Their own eyes droop downward and they seem to have gotten smaller. One child even sits down again, then lies dramatically on her side, until the man nudges her with his foot.

"It's too hot," she says. "I'm boiling!" The child drops her head to one side, lets her tongue hang.

"Knock it off," the man says.

"Don't you want to play?" Carol says to the child on the ground, weakly, begging. She was better at this last year.

"Only if you close your eyes," Conner says, then chants, "Close your eyes! Close your eyes!" The man takes Conner by the arm, shushing him.

"No, it's okay, you're right. You know why? Because we have to imagine it's nighttime, and it's too dark to see the moths." She closes her eyes.

She imagines tiny sand-brown moths fluttering in the orange halo of a street light, smacking against the plexiglass cover, falling away, and fluttering back. But there are moths in the dark, too, swirling in random patterns in the trees alongside the lake, unaware of the bats that flood from the old shed every night at dusk. Dark shapes clumped at the gap above the shed window, then flapped away, silhouetted only briefly against the navy sky, then obscured completely by the forest of white pine, blue spruce and cedar at the edge of their suburb. Olivia claimed to name them all, made a list, began a catalogue of portraits, never finished because the bats left, school resumed that fall and there were other things she had to do. Even a child must prioritize things, let the unnecessary joys fall away.

"Bat," Carol says, and her voice sounds surreally close. The vibrations in her cheeks and nose make her conscious that she does not really know the sound of her own voice—it is always in front of a fleshy wall of resonance. She imagines her nose like a little brown bat's, like that of a little dog, pointed and dark. They sing from the mouth.

"Moth," children whisper. One girl is somewhere to Carol's right and she can hear her footsteps shuffling along the grass as if she could disguise herself with unusual walking. It sounds like she is following the circumference of the circle. Another child is behind her and Carol turns around, but as she does, she hears the child swoop past to the other side of the circle. Close to her left now, a child whispers sh, sh, sh, like the wind, then giggles.

"Bat," she says again, steps lightly in front of her, then takes a step back. She will confuse them with her haphazard directions. Moth, moth, moth. More bodies circling her, laughing, a carousel of sound. Eventually, a child will give itself up willingly, stay in one place as she approaches, arms folded around itself, giggling, pretending to fear the bat, but really wanting to be caught, to be the special moth that is eaten first.

"Bat." The wind gets up and moves behind Carol, sh, sh, sh.

Carol can feel the heat from another body ahead of her—someone is crouching. "Moth," the child whispers. Carol steps forward, eyes shut tight. It feels like she is near the edge of the circle, like she may stumble over a bean bag any moment and she steps cautiously, too first to make sure she is still on solid ground. Olivia was always tired after a tour. Everything is fine, Mom.

"Bat."

When she sang—something so pure must be joyous.

"Moth."

The circle is larger than Carol remembers—she has not reached the edge yet. But where is this child? Is she on the other side? But someone would have said something, Conner would have pointed out a cheater. You're not lying to me, are you?

"Bat."

"Moth."

She is below Carol, but so far below it sounds like she is calling up to her from some watery darkness. They say the heart stops before you hit the water, but this is not a comfort—that she was already gone. That she was gone before she hit the water, sunk in the cold, down, past barnacled rocks and kelp and spider crabs, rock fish and shiners, down, through marine snow, dinoflagellates and copepods, down, past purple star fish and sun stars and anemones, down, urchins and rock crabs and Dungeness, down, out, carried away by a tide, down, decaying, disappearing in the cold piece by piece, washing up somewhere one day as a shoe tangled up in sun-dried sea weed, she can't let that happen but it will, but she can't let that happen. Everything is fine, Mom. Carol bends her knees, hands in front fluttering toward the heat, slowly, slowly, and the other moths have gone quiet and even the wind has stopped, and Carol wonders if they have all gone now, if she were to open her eyes would they be gone?

"Bat," she whispers.

Nothing comes back.

"Olivia?"

Then, very faintly, as if the grass itself were speaking to her, "Moth."

"Are you there?" Carol calls, her voice breaking, her nose tingling and her stomach vibrating now, trying hard to contain the images that swell up from deep inside.

She wasn't there to witness it, but she sees Olivia on that night: A shadowy silhouette, tiny, far away, and spinning as she falls, rigidly splayed like a plastic doll.

Or the water below, black, only the crests of wind-blown waves visible now and then for the phosphorescence, like teeth under a black light.

Or Olivia's face, her lips puckered in concentration, large hazel eyes with blonde-tipped lashes, always more expressive than they needed to be, widening with surprise, squinting with concentration, but with a stillness in her pupils now that seems to contradict any feeling at all. She sees her face, damp in the autumn humidity and Olivia is not crying. She is on the outside of the bridge now, hands clasping the rail behind her. She is not feeling in this moment, only thinking. Feeling is already gone. Then Olivia turns toward her, resolved, whispers a final exhale, closes her eyes.

Carol flutters down, clasps the soft arm, sobs.

The little girl with the black pigtails lies flat on her back, staring at Carol, no longer smiling, and her nanny crouches down just outside the circle.

"I'm sorry," Carol says, squeezes her eyes shut.

"Come on, let's go," the nanny says softly. Carol lets go of the girl's arm, feels the heat going away from her as the girl steps outside the circle. She can hear others gathering bags and moving away.

In a moment, when everyone has gone, she will get up. For now, she keeps her eyes closed. "I'm sorry," she says again. Waits for the sound to come back.

Dog

I came to this campground to get away from the mess in my apartment, half-gutted now that Tara was moving out. I won't be sorry
to see the "fine art" go, like the Georgia O'Keeffe images on cheap
glossy paper and black and white photos of women's bodies twined
together. Or Tara's books: *The Joy of Lesbian Sex*, like some compul-
sory manual she's supposed to have. *The Well of Loneliness*, another
item as standard as a dictionary in the lives of my ex-girlfriends, and
just as seldom consulted. The dog, a shelter dog that was labelled
"Shepherd X" behind its bars the day Tara got it, silent, mopey eyes
staring up at her. "As long as I don't have to look after it," I'd said.
"Fine by me."

After a few days of stepping around boxes and garbage bags
of clothes, I said, "I should leave—I'll just go camp somewhere for
a few days."

"Maybe that will help," Tara said, as if reassuring me.

"I don't need help."

"Fine," she said. "Then at least take the dog with you. I'm
going to be busy moving."

She always wants too much. But I'm done with that now. I
came here because who needs it? I can be alone—an ascetic. Eat less,
and whatever I do eat, serve it up plain, like the can of chickpeas I
had for dinner last night, or the raw carrots I gnawed all morning to
stave off hunger. I wandered up the beach to keep the boredom at
bay, like another whining dog. Down, boredom, down! But I would
kill for a cup of coffee. Not that I expected this to be easy. I'm sure
it's a process, a day by day shedding of old skins. In a surprising way,
I'm not completely hating the dog's company, but it's difficult not
to be distracted by the other people here—the butch in one trailer,
the man with the two kids in the other, who I'm trying to avoid.

He already hates me. First, the dog peed on his tarp, not ten minutes after I arrived, which was tucked neatly below his trailer hitch. I was not far away, setting up my tent at the time. "Put your dog on a leash," he said. Then the shit thing.

After some canned corn and unsalted soda crackers at lunch, there is nothing left to do but sit in the tent, full of dog breath now. I'm a cheese, smoked in canine stench. I take a sock off and pick at my big toe nail. There's dirt under all my nails. "I bet you'd like to lick this raunchy foot," I say to the dog at the other end of the sleep-ing bag, who smacks its tongue and sighs.

So I spy on the butch woman through the screen window. The dog breathes audibly, sometimes lifting its head when a twig snaps, or a tree creaks in the wind from the ocean. At these mo-ments, I shush the dog, as if its curiosity could blow my cover. Then I turn back to watch the woman. She sits in a lawn chair, sipping a bottle of beer in front of the fire.

I'd noticed her campsite first. There was a mosaic of cracked clam shells that collected beside the fire pit, the little cream-coloured trailer that looked like a prehistoric egg on two wheels, red pick-up truck. Judging from the burnt-orange pine needles on the hood of the truck, she'd been at the campground for a while. Later that day, I met her in the bathroom. She was scrubbing her teeth like she was sanding paint off. Her hair was wet and combed back so that it took on a fifties look. She would look great in a white T-shirt with a packet of cigarettes rolled up in one sleeve, strutting defiantly down some urban street, ready to fight or fall in love.

I smiled, said faintly, "Hi."

The woman nodded, spat, drank from the tap, gargled, and spat again. "That's better," she announced, glancing at me in the mirror. She had a small mouth, which didn't seem to match the forceful way she moved. She squeezed some cream into one palm, rubbed her hands together as if she was trying to get warm, then slapped them on her freckled cheeks before smearing. In the bathroom's fluorescent light, my coloured hair changed from strawberry-auburn to plasticky-orange against my skin, so it washed my light brown complexion into a greenish hue. I was taller than her, just like I'm taller than most women, my shoulders too broad and the backs of my arms covered in tiny pink dots, like pimples, but it's just irritated skin. Maybe it's toxins. But the woman didn't seem to notice any of this. She squinted as she smiled, like offering a conspiratorial invitation. This could be a roadside bathroom, this woman a truck driver with six more hours of nighttime driving before she calls it a night. I was a lone traveller headed the same direction. Two separate people in the night—would that be so hard?

The woman threw her towel over one shoulder and as she left, said, "Don't worry, I saved some hot water for ya!"

"Thanks!" I said as the door swung shut. I held my hand under the shower, waited for it to heat up from gardenhose-cold to a tolerable lukewarm, and got in. I imagined she hadn't left. She would walk toward my shower stall and pause outside, her feet in black thongs pointing at me under the door. I would turn the lock, the metal post screeching out of its hole, echoing in the concrete bathroom. She would smile when I opened the door, to signify her intent, to make it playful and innocent, and then I would smile, too, before we became serious again. She'd step into the stall, lock the door behind her, grab my waist, kiss me on the mouth. With my eyes closed, I could be anyone, and then I'd realize I'd been holding my breath because now my tits against her tits, now the water, and there is hot water—oh yes, here comes the hot water! I thought I heard the dog moan outside, but I'd sighed at the same time, so I wasn't sure if it was just the sound of my own voice bouncing strangely around the tiles, or if the dog was up to something. The hot water cooled. It would get cold soon and I hadn't even shampooed.

So much had not happened between us, and I'd only just arrived that morning.

That was a few days ago. Since then, I've eaten three cans

of chickpeas, the corn, a pound of carrots, a box of unsalted soda crackers, and a giant bag of trail mix—first the Smarties, then the cashews, almonds, raisins, and finally, peanuts. Why do they put so many peanuts in trail mix? I thought about counting them before I ate, but that bored me, too. I even read a Harlequin romance I found in the bathroom, though I wanted to empty my mind. Clean house.

"I should be like you," I say to the dog. "Vacuous." It's hard not to think about Tara.

The woman leans over one side of her chair, and when she sits up again, she twists a cap off a new bottle, and then slaps her leg. Maybe a mosquito. There could be a raindrop-sized splatter of blood there now, a black smear, too, then the itch.

"Your mom is a mosquito," I say to the dog. It raises its head. I try to pat it on the forehead, but it licks at my forearm. "You want a beer?" Maybe we could join the woman. Kill time.

What if I unleash the dog? It might go after the squirrel that had started cheeping somewhere in the dusk out there. I could traipse after it with a flashlight, pausing to ask the woman, "Have you seen a shepherd cross go by?"

I told Tara the dog was her problem.

"We got him together," she said, pleading.

"Not really." Separate bills, separate rent, and definitely separate dog. Why was that too much?

"But he'll be good for you—dogs are honest and they love people," she said. Subtle.

At first it was easy with Tara. She'd confessed her attraction to me one summer afternoon. The balcony door was open, so all we heard was the leaves in the oaks and the newspaper on the table as the wind lifted a corner now and then. She was tying her shoe as if she was ready to leave. She spoke to the floor and I smiled at her discomfort, elated that I had the power to absolve her. "Me too," I said. I liked how new she was at this. Could I ever look so relieved as she did in that moment? She moved in with me. Was it only a year

JANE AND THE WHALES

ago? She made friends with my friends, or not my friends, really. I was as interested in them as I was *The Well of Loneliness*; that is to say, they bored me. But Tara volunteered at the community dances, wore boas and black leather at the Pride stuff, had groups of four or five over for dinner. They gossiped, drank wine, and laced every-thing they said with sexual innuendo until someone would finally be blunt, talk about eating pussy, and they'd laugh. Then they would go out. I retrieved crackers from kitchen cupboards without making a sound, hoping to go undetected. I imagined them, a pack out on the town, sniffing around for mates. What a disappointment. She went to Las Vegas for a week with the girls and I felt relieved.

"Fine. I'll take the dog." Probably owed her that.

She sat on the couch and rubbed her face with her hands. The dog rested its head on her knee. "Thank you," she said, stroking its forehead.

If the dog is so keen on loving people, it would find its own way to the woman's fire. Bonus for me, because I could trot in after it, say, "Oh, there you are," laugh, tie the yellow rope on its collar. But I couldn't risk having the dog revisit the other trailer.

Earlier, I watched the man open the door of his fifth wheel with his foot, carrying out a couple bowls of cereal in one hand, a pink jug in the other, and a few cups wedged in his elbow out to his little girls. "Who's ready for juice?" he said. He asked them who's up for a boat ride. The little one raised her hand. The dad smiled, then scanned the campground until he noticed me. I checked to make sure the dog was still attached to the yellow rope and noticed it was in the middle of defecating, its back arched and hind tucked under. I patted my pockets, pretending to search for a plastic bag. I was going to whack the poo into some salal with a stick, but now there was a witness.

The dad thumped into the trailer again and returned with a plastic grocery bag, crossing the gravel road toward me.

"I got one," he offered, annoyed.

"Thanks," I said.

"Do you need more? I don't want my kids running into dog shit around here."

"No—that's okay, I have some, just not on me. I forgot." The dad walked back to the picnic table without saying anything else.

I decide to lie down and close my eyes. The pillow smells like ocean, sand, pine, dirt. I can't stretch out with the dog at the end of the bag. Of course, I never got used to sharing. That's why I had the foamy under the bed, something I could pull out easily. I didn't mind the floor. So at least tent-life is comfortable enough for me, this same foamy, this same bag, just more fresh air. I could take that bed to the dump. I could just have this foamy in an empty room. Float on the carpet. I could rip up the carpet. Concrete. Cold floor feels clean, aseptic. I could sit quietly there, white walls, soundproof it.

The dog wakes me in the middle of the night, chirping and jolting its paws. The dog has moved up and is lying beside me now, its nose nearly to mine. "He's chasing rabbits," Tara would have said. Then she would have imitated the dog, lain side by side, a pair of jiggling commas. As I inhale, the dog exhales, so I am breathing in its dogbreath, this horrible figure eight of used breath, so all those clean air molecules have passed over its gums and rough tongue and yellowing molars which I had seen eat a block-hard piece of shit once, then down its dog throat, lungs, blood, back, out those wet nostrils and into me. I sit up, and as my eyes adjust to the dark, stroke the dog's face until its chirping stops and it raises its head lazily. I can't see clearly in the dark, but I'm sure the dog is looking at me. It's easier when you can't see them. Maybe it's having one of those honest and people-loving moments.

I say, "You're a good dog, I guess." It heaves a breath that sounds impatient, or sad, or satisfied, the way Tara did that night we broke up. I had the foamy on the living room floor, to give her privacy, but she got up for glasses of water, trips to the bathroom, took a shower at midnight, even left the apartment in pajamas.

She came back a few minutes later. "What are you doing?" I said.

"Checking the mail!"

"Just go to sleep—I'll forward it for you."

I could hear her just standing in the hall, probably waiting for me to add a little something. Maybe, "I'm sorry—I'll always love you." Or, "Maybe I should leave—you keep the apartment." After all, I was the one who'd ended it. But it was my apartment.

"You think I'm an asshole," I say to the dog. It doesn't say anything back. It seems to be asleep again.

~

In the morning, I wake up because something is pushing on my bladder. The dog is on all fours, pointing its nose at the tent zipper, its rear paw digging into me.

"Fine, fine," I say, and pull my jeans on over yesterday's underwear. Maybe it's all this attending to the dog that is getting in the way of my Zen. In some places, people do tai chi early in the morning because the trees give off the best energy at that time. I use this mystical hour to pick up the dog's first bowel movements.

I take the yellow rope I use to tie up the foamy and attach one end to the dog's collar. Tara offered me a dog leash, but I had no intention of "walking a dog" on this trip. "Don't look at me. It's not my fault you peed on the tarp." The dog lowers its head and white crescents appear as it looks up at me, so that its eyes seem larger and rounder than they usually do. I make a mopey face back, pouting my lower lip out, but I do feel a little bad for making fun. All it's got is the body, and not even that.

When I start walking, the dog trots ahead until the rope tugs, then it pauses to sniff, raises one leg and urinates on a fawn lily. It keeps going until the fawn lily droops under the weight of this shower, and I have to pee now, too. The bathrooms are across the campground, but I have to pee so bad now I'm getting stabbing pains in the bladder. I cross my legs, push my fist into my groin, but I have to pee. The dog squints lazily like this feels so good. "When did you drink so much water!" I say. I can't take it, so I pull my jeans down and squat in the salal, just behind a fir tree so I'm out of sight. And it's weird, but so typical, because I don't even pee right away, just squat there, waiting with this stabbing pain and burning sensation, looking at the dirt beneath me, willing it to turn into a puddle. "Come on!" Then it comes.

"Sweet relief!" I say. The dog comes over to me and licks my face. "Get out of here!" It wanders away, dragging the yellow rope in the dirt. I keep my eyes on it so it doesn't make a mess out there. It stops to sniff as it approaches the dad who is straight ahead of me.

"This is the trail," he says, pointing down. He takes the dog's leash like now it's under control, like now he can reel this in, but tosses it back like an empty net, and walks away.

I get my pants on and yank the dog over. "You're gross," I say. I feel guilty about this comment almost immediately. I'd seen the dog with Tara and how much it loved her, or wanted love from her, often walking up to her to lick her jeans, or her cheek when she offered it. What if I bring it back as damaged goods, emotionally neglected and distant? Maybe this is what had happened with Tara. We didn't seem to cross paths in the kitchen as often, or end up brushing our teeth at the same time. After my own mother mistook my voice on the phone for Tara's, I figured I could use a little more space. Of course I didn't wonder if she really wanted to go to Las Vegas.

"Go. Stay. I could care less."

The dog glances back at me, pausing for a moment.

"I wasn't talking to you."

The woman is sitting in her chair, smoking, with a Thermos tucked between her legs. She leans back as she exhales, and looks up at the pine tree that towers over her campsite. She opens the Thermos and takes a sip from the steaming container.

"Nice leash!" she calls.

"Thanks." I raise the rope to display it. "It's an antique." What a terrible joke. That wasn't me, was it?

"I can see that," she says. "Bring that dog over here. I wanna meet the little shit disturber."

Had she found the dog's shit, too? The woman places her Thermos on the trailer step and her cigarette in one side of her mouth, and then calls through the other side to the dog, patting her thighs and bending over. "Come 'ere, boy!"

I drop the rope and the dog runs to the woman.

"Or girl—nope, boy. There ya go."

The dog wags its tail, nosing her hands, licking her fingers. What had she touched today? Coffee? Her truck? Hands washed with dish soap—lemon, WD-40, salty wrists, skin sweet and oily like peanuts and dried apples, and the tangy, scorched scent of tobacco on fingers.

The dog nuzzles her crotch. "You got a crotch-dog, eh?"

"Sorry." I pick up the rope again.

"That's okay!" she says to the dog, holding its jowls in her hands. "Ya pooper dog!" She punctuates this greeting with a pat on its head, then sits down again, reaching behind her to grab the Thermos. "Guy over there actually complained to me about your dog. He's been here a couple weeks now so he thinks he lives here. Like you been shitting in his backyard, ya know?"

"I know. Sorry." I don't know if she's lecturing me, or complaining about being put in the middle of a dispute, or just talking about the dog. "It's a friend's dog."

"Well, he is cute." As she inhales a drag of her cigarette, she squints with one eye, smiling. "Where you from?" The sun is peeking through the trees so that one side of her face is spotlighted. I must be a silhouette with the sun behind me like this. The woman won't be able to see me, or where I'm looking. Her eyes are green with flecks of brown, which makes her look unpredictable, as if even her body is undecided on how to express itself. She would be free-spirited, untameable …

"Not quite awake yet, eh?"

"Sorry," I say. "Just drifted."

"Want some coffee?"

I would kill for a coffee.

She points with her thumb to the trailer. "Only take me a minute." She leans forward with her hands on the arms of the chair, reinforcing how easy this would be, how she is now already halfway to the coffee, and I just had to say the word. Say, Yes, I want that. She hovers there a moment, as if I have the power to unlock her. She is frozen in time, preserved. Her trailer is dimpled with years of use. She could be a perpetual traveller, earning a living off royalties from hit songs she wrote in the seventies. She'd have a Mexican blanket on the bed, a shaggy bath mat. She'd put coffee on and I would sit on the bed, which would be right beside the stove. This handsome butch would sit beside me while we waited for the kettle to boil. She'd say, "Lie back, I want to show you something," then plug something in. Then the ceiling would light up with coloured Christmas lights. She'd put on a record, because she would have a record player—even though it had to sit on the floor anytime she listened to music—because records have the warm sound, with a steady stream of breath like an exhale through rounded lips, and textured with wear. It would be one of her songs, and without saying anything, I'd turn my head to look at her and she would know that was an invitation, and lie on top of me, pushing her thigh against my crotch, then wet lips on my neck.

"I have to go into town for some things." The words pop out.

She sinks back into her chair. "Town! What do you need from town? We got the whole bounty of the ocean at our feet." She pats the dog, smearing her hand over its brow with such force, it looks like she might peel its face right off. But the dog loves it, inching closer between pats. "I'm going crabbing in a bit. Those suckers are all over the place, just hiding in the sand."

"Do you need a licence for that?"

"Probably. You won't tell on me, will ya?" She winks. She stops patting the dog to take another sip from her Thermos. The dog noses her hand, demanding more affection.

"You want me to lie for you?" Was I being funny? My voice sounds so low, like I'm dead serious. Was this seductive? Probably not.

The dog jumps up so its paws rest on her thighs, and licks her face. "Sorry." I fumble toward the rope to pull it away.

The woman grabs its front legs, lifting them down so the dog is on all fours again. "He's fine, he's fine." She leans back, resting one leg on the other, ankle to the knee. Her dark leg hair peeks out from her jeans, wool socks with a red band across the top. A Mountain Woman. She could build us a fire, sweaty in a greying tank, dark nipples visible through thinning cotton.

The dog is excited now, sitting on its haunches, tail sweeping the dirt, whole body wiggling, then licking its mouth, swallowing. Its penis, normally just a furry pouch, is red and shiny now, like a skinned finger pointing.

"Hey—no!" I yank its collar, but it only readjusts, persists.

"He's fine," the woman says again. "We've all been there—well, not there, exactly" she laughs, glancing down at the dog's erection. "But close enough."

But I grab its collar and pull until the dog is down on the ground, and say, "Bad dog! Bad dog!" My hand around its throat, pushing each time I said bad, until the dog stops smiling, its eyes darting now and then to mine, but looking quickly away, ashamed. I let go of the collar.

"You said he's a friend's dog?"

She almost sounds concerned the way she asks this, slowly and softly, as if it has a complicated answer. When I look up, her eyes are searching me. "I'm sorry," I say. "I don't really know anything about dogs."

She takes another drag of her cigarette, nodding and laughing as she exhales. "Oh, you're fine. Just remember—dogs are people, too. Know what I mean?"

"Thanks," I say. Then add, "Nice talking to you."

The woman says, "Sure," and pats the dog once more, much gentler than she had before.

I stop midway back to my tent. Should I turn around, say, "I'm sorry," and explain: this isn't my dog, I've just gone through a breakup, stress or something, and actually, I would like a cup of coffee? Endure whatever I say after that: where one finds a good cup of coffee, mundane observations about the benefits of spending time in the woods, Tara, love notes on the fridge, visits to other people's parents, five-year-plans. But why tread water in the same eddy? Forget it. I want to lie down in my tent now. I must have slept wrong because my neck hurts, like I've got a bruise twisted around it. "This is probably your fault," I say, but the dog ignores me.

I open another can of chickpeas. My fork has a bit of sand and dog hair stuck to it, so I rinse it over my fire pit, and eat the peas one at a time, to make it take longer. I sit on the ground, beside the tent, so the woman and the dad and the kids won't be able to see me over here, eating my cold can of food. They wouldn't understand that this is why I'm here. Simplify, desire nothing. Easy to do when the only option tastes like this. And I declined coffee. I'm making progress. But soon the chickpeas are gone. I empty the juice into the fire pit, let it drool out of the can, and put the can in the garbage bag in my car, which is beginning to smell sour, the drops of pea juice fermenting. Now nothing until dinner. "Get in the tent," I say. The dog and I lie down.

I think of the woman, maybe in her trailer now, cooking up something good. She'll have some signature thing she makes—maybe it's pasta, with spinach and a surprise wad of mozzarella in the centre. Maybe she makes a great chicken curry, with Sri Lankan spices— bay leaves, cinnamon, black curry powder. She could be cooking it right now, letting it stew, soaking in the flavour, until the flesh and everything else absorbs the things around it. She could be lying down, too, top off, breasts lolling to the side, because it would be hot in her trailer. She wouldn't use AC. She could be loosening her belt, unbuttoning her jeans, hands down her men's underwear, the pouch just more room for her to move around, circling her clitoris, imagining me on her bed, mouth to her pussy, swirling my tongue and sucking, and sucking like she's filling my mouth, swollen and pulsing, wet. She tastes salty like the ocean, as if she's been wading in the water, slippery as kelp, and I'm sucking on her like I need her to breathe, she is oxygen, she is food and water, she is breath-ing hard, she is moaning—sweet moaning—and my hand is rubbing hard, my hand is rubbing like I'm trying to start a fire, my wrist is sore but I keep going, quiet, closer, like the tide is rising, up to my neck, my mouth, my nose, until I have to hold my breath, hold it, hold—let it go. Release. Sink.

When I open my eyes, the dog is looking right at me. I sudden-ly feel horrible, as though I've molested the dog. It keeps looking at me, as if it were about to ask a question. "Just say it," I say. "What?"

The dog just watches me.

"What?"

Although it does not move a muscle, I can see it thinking, judging me.

"Fine, I'm a hypocrite."

The dog begins to drool. It might have looked hungry, but its eyes are soft, sad almost, the eye brows tilted down at the sides, its lids drooping.

"What do you want me to do about it?"

The dog does not move.

"Are you sleep-walking or something?" I snap my fingers. The sleeping bag is turning dark where the drool spreads. "I'm not going to listen to something that can't even control its own saliva produc-tion. Look at that! Look what you're doing to my bag!"

Nothing.

"Speak!" I say. The dog barks twice. Then it rushes at me, pushing me down with its forelegs. It lies on top of me, its elbows digging into my ribs, its claws at my neck. When I breathe, I inhale the dog's own breath again, its leathery nose so close to mine I can feel the humidity of it, the drool on my throat, then down the sides of my neck.

"You're crushing me!" The dog could sink right into me, turn me into a puddle, lick me up, chew my bones. "You'd like to crush me, wouldn't you?" I push the dog to the side. "Lie down!" I say, and bury my face into the pillow.

I remember in bed one night, before Las Vegas, sun dimming behind the curtain, faces flushed, soft eyes, lips red and hot, sweet smell of pussy, a different feeling—rolling underneath. Hands pawed at my cheek and patted damp hair from my forehead. I love you I love you I love you, of course—yes. But something else, too. "You're a part of me," she said, wrapped her hands around my head, pulled me closer. "And I'm a part of you." Smiled. I smiled back. She looked so happy, so maybe I did too. I turned to see us in the full-length mirror. Her arms round me, octopus. My arms, thick as snakes. I could slither around her, twist her up like a boa, take her in. Is this what she wants? We could dissolve in our own saliva. Or I could turn me inside out, my fat flesh disintegrating, Tara jumping back, consoling herself, collapsing into a rosy mess, and me: red, just muscles, bones.

I got up. "Where are you going?" Tara asked.

My neck felt wet—sweat? "I'll be right back." Wash.

There is nothing to do but sleep. The hours are too empty here. I'm getting bitten. The dad hates me. I'm wasting my time. I'm trying to get perspective, but I can't get any perspective, not with my face in this pillow and my body in this hot tent. I look at the dog. It lies down, groans, black eyebrows moving up and down, one at a time. It's worried, but it looks around the tent so I won't think it's just watching me, but I know because I'm worried, too. Maybe I'm just hungry.

"I guess I should feed you," I say to the dog. I reach for my jeans and push the sleeping bag down. Sand, dirt, and a spray of dog hair stick to my legs and stomach. I try to brush it off but it just sticks there. I pinch one hair at a time, and then flick it at the dog. "You're everywhere," I say.

I touch my own hair, which feels thick with salt and dust from the packed dirt around the campsite. Hadn't I just showered that morning? But that was days ago, and since then, I've been all the same places as the dog, through the trails flanked with salal and sword ferns, and the beach with that foul smell of gull-cracked oyster shells, and into the ocean, into that blend of seaweed, decay-ing mammals and vegetation, blooms of fish semen or something, algae- cloaked Dungeness, then wet dog, salt hair, and we've circled this place again and again. There's nowhere left to go. So who cares? I could go out just like this, naked, roll around in the beds of dried kelp, hopping with sand fleas. I could run past that picnic table with the man and his kids, steal wieners from their hotdog buns, or whine outside the woman's trailer, piss on the tires of her truck, wait, wait, wait. I'd probably get the place to myself.

But I wonder if I could make it to the car and back with a bowl of dog food.

Other People's Houses

Tom Douglas had only become interested in constructing birdhouses after purchasing the Travis Street property. There was something in the way the cedars and Douglas firs shadowed the surrounding lawns, towering over them, which needed to be civilized: a single story A-frame here, a simple dormer there. He had constructed the first houses for northern flickers, made one rectangular box with a roof that sloped downward from the rear side. He painted it red with white trim, like a country barn, and mounted it on a snag at the end of the driveway. But he never saw a flicker at the box. European starlings invaded the home instead, asserting themselves with high-pitched whistles. Tom knew the difference between a good bird and an invasive species, as did everyone these days. His wife, Beverly, had even made a donation to a local environmental organization. Got their names on the website. So Tom dusted rat poison and bug killer into the house, then tossed the dead chicks into the garbage, along with the dismantled house the following week. It might have been a gruesome task, but Tom felt so much sympathy for the woodpeckers and other indigenous birds whose homes were snatched up by these invaders. From then on, he had made houses for flycatchers and nut-hatches only, the holes too small for starlings to enter.

As he stared out the front window surveying a location for his next house, his daughter, Carla, arrived home with her friend Bonnie. It was a terribly inconvenient weekend for this Bonnie girl to stay here. Tom's new Authentic Italian Brick Oven had arrived earlier in the week, and he was christening it tomorrow with a pork shank roast. He'd invited two couples—Beverly's friends mostly—because he knew this would compel Beverly to attend.

"Welcome, Bonnie," Tom said as the girls entered. "You can put your shoes in the hall closet."

Bonnie pulled her shoes off by stepping on each heel, her long black hair curtaining her face. When she looked up again, Tom thought he recognized her. Her narrow, hooked nose seemed at odds with her high cheekbones and wide, black eyes, and there was something owl-like in her appearance.

"Carla tells me your mother is out of town."

"She's picking mushrooms," Carla explained.

Two days was a long time to leave a child with another man's family, Tom thought. "Is there some way we can reach her in case of emergency?"

Bonnie looked to Carla, who said, as if translating, "Dory doesn't have a cellphone."

"Dory?" Tom said. "That's your mother?" Is that the same woman he'd met at the PTA meeting last year, when Beverly couldn't go? The one who slouched in her chair, long crinkled skirt and crocheted vest, some terrible throwback to the sixties, and slurped tea from a thermos? At the break, she hovered by the Dutch gingersnaps Beverly had bought for Tom to bring, wiping crumbs from her face with her sleeve.

"These are divine," she'd said about the store-bought cookies. She might have looked like a scavenger if Tom hadn't been distracted by the way her breasts hung low and loose beneath her cotton blouse. This reminded Tom of a girl in high school who'd dance with him by spinning and spinning with her eyes closed.

"I see," Tom said. But this was very unseemly. The last time he'd seen that woman they'd shared a joint behind the school, after the PTA meeting. Shared a little more than that. But it was over almost as quickly as it began—a matter of minutes. It was as casual, as trivial an act as a couple of mating sparrows. But she wasn't coming until Sunday, so Tom decided not to worry.

"I'm making baked spaghetti for dinner, so please don't snack beforehand."

"Okay, Dad!" Carla tugged Bonnie upstairs. Bonnie smiled,

and Tom smiled back before he noticed the mustard stain on the sleeve of Bonnie's shirt, and saw in its muddied shape the boiled wieners of his own childhood, minute rice, and fluorescent orange macaroni. He picked up Bonnie's shoes to place them neatly inside the closet. They were canvas slip-on things, the white rubber stained to grey and the red canvas faded, a hole nearly worn where her big toe would be. Bonnie's mother probably bought shoes in the same place she purchased groceries. He should feel sorry for her— that's what Beverly would do. But Tom chose self-discpline and law school, while Bonnie's mother chose mushroom picking. Why should he pity her poor choices?

The girls thumped loudly upstairs. "What in hell?" he said. He might have worried someone had fallen, except he had gotten used to this new regimen of obnoxious behaviour. Carla was only ten and already a phone hog, too. She'd even suggested getting her own line. "And how about a secretary?" Tom had teased, but he must have said it too quick, or too hard, because Carla had simply muttered, "Sorry," and left the room. She used to think he was funny, but all of Beverly's criticism was making it difficult to retain his good sense of humour. She was the one who'd left, but even so, he felt like a guest in his own home.

Tom went out to the backyard to check the temperature of his Authentic Italian Brick Oven: an immovable steel stand, terracotta dome stained peach with a nuanced tone, handmade. The new oven needed five days to properly prepare it for use, eliminating moisture from inside the dome. He fired it the day after Beverly left. Today was the fifth day and the temperature was at 300 degrees Fahrenheit. Tomorrow, it would be ready for the pork shank roast. He would roast a leg of pork the way people might have done a thousand years ago. Food today was substandard. He would explain to Beverly about additives, colours and preservatives, and the mechanical processes that dilute the real flavours. He'd even had to visit several butchers to track down a leg of pork with the skin on.

Most of the ham was sliced into cold cuts, and many of the roasts were tenderloins, the fat sliced away and the skin removed. He liked pork skin, too, the way it browned and cracked. He could snap a piece off and dip it in the soft fat. His own mother had preferred to feed him meats that were reshaped, unrecognizable, like spam, meatloaf, minced fish sticks and chicken fingers.

"Chickens," he said aloud, "do not have fingers." Then he looked up at Carla's dormer window where Bonnie's reckless mane whipped in circles inside. What is that—dancing? Carla probably found this humorous, but if they tried to pull some stunt out here tomorrow, he'd slingshot a stern look her way, and she'd take the antics upstairs.

Tom glanced around the backyard, making note of the things he could count on: the iron patio furniture—he will get the cushions from the garage; the glass table—Windex; get Carla to sweep. The birdhouses added an almost whimsical touch to the scene. The combination of iron, forest, and little houses reminded Tom of a fairy tale. But the house in the fir at the rear of the yard looked like it was missing its perch. Strange, Tom thought. Perhaps Beverly had done it, some vindictive and petty act, although how she got the perch out—which was glued into its hole—he wasn't sure. Did she get up there with a saw? He would have to make a new perch, use more glue, really jam it in there.

~

Soon, the smells of stewed tomatoes, garlic, onion, basil and olive oil wafted through the house. Tom tapped on Carla's door. "Girls, it's time to set the table."

"Coming!" Carla chimed. Tom went downstairs, leaned against the kitchen counter, and flipped through the latest *National Geographic*: red pandas, long-horned beetles eating away trees, Indian stupas with people walking in circles. Circumambulation, it was called. He was happy to learn the correct word. He'd bought the lifetime subscription, and had filled two shelves with issues so far.

"How do you know you'll get your money's worth?" Beverly had teased.

"What do you mean?"

"If we die tomorrow, you will have overpaid."

Tom didn't smoke, drank only moderately, never ate processed foods. His own father had lived until eighty-five, and he had been a drunk. Pathetic. Killed his mother, basically, because she had to pick up the slack, and after all that, he still managed to complain to Tom that life had treated him unfairly. "What did you ever do to deserve anything?" Tom had said. When he'd told Beverly about this, she shook her head. "He did put a roof over your head," she said. "Don't be so petty." This was the same woman who was gifted a trip to Europe simply for graduating high school.

Carla showed Bonnie where they kept the silverware, then placed three matching plates on the table, and a white linen serviette beside each one. Bonnie put the forks and knives together in pairs beside each plate.

"No, no, no." Carla clicked her tongue in mock disapproval. "Forks on the left, knives on the right, blade turned in, a big spoon for the spaghetti."

"Yeah, right, I'm gonna eat spaghetti with a spoon." Bonnie curtseyed. "A spoon for me, sir, for I am a la-ady." Then she sang, "La-dee-da, la-dee-dee, I eat spaghetti, birds sing!"

Carla snorted. Then, as Bonnie held a pinky to her mouth, Carla snatched her hand, and said, "Oh my God, you need to wash your hands."

Tom flipped absently through his magazine as the girls slammed the door to the bathroom, followed by an eruption of laughter. Carla was getting louder every year. The tap ran. "Look at your nails!" Carla shouted, followed by a ghost-like "Oooo" from Bonnie.

"Scrub those nails, you little pig!" Carla laughed.

Tom flipped the pages. The pagodas are often secular places now in China. Some stupas hold relics of the Buddha, toes and fingers.

The Douglas family did not say grace at the beginning of every supper. Grace was reserved for holidays, or when company was over. Sometimes Tom invited Carla's friends to say grace if they wanted. Most of them shook their heads shyly, "No, thanks, Mr. Douglas." So he did it. Carla's mother never liked to say grace because she did not believe in God. Neither did Tom, so this phony display often led to an argument before bed. Bonnie's mother probably thanked the creator, or the goddess or the universe for their tuna casserole or pizza pockets.

"Bonnie, would you like to say grace?" Tom asked.

Bonnie held Carla's hand and bowed her head, almost to her plate, so that the shaggy fringe of her black hair touched it. "Dear God: Rub-a-dub-dub, thanks for the grub. The End."

"Amen," Tom said.

Carla laughed. "Amen."

Tom took the ladle that lay beside the spaghetti dish. "This isn't an appropriate tool for spaghetti. Where are the spaghetti tongs?"

"In the dishwasher," Carla said.

"Then wash them."

While Carla disappeared to retrieve the tongs, Bonnie picked at her fingers under the table. Tom resisted the temptation to scold her for this. He never invited her here. Regardless, he aimed to dem-onstrate polite hospitality. "It is not income that determines class," he liked to say, "but class." After buying the stone lions for the end of the driveway, Beverly told him it was not overpriced ornaments that determined class, either.

When Carla returned with the tongs, she nudged Bonnie, glancing at her hands and smiling, as if they had just shared a private joke. Tom wondered if what few manners she retained would be undone by Bonnie, like the buttons of a shirt, until she was naked, a fleshy pink animal whispering private jokes and mopping up sauce with a crust of bread.

He served the girls their portions, adding a sprig of fresh basil to each plate. Bonnie clasped her fork like a shovel and scooped a pile of noodles into her mouth. As she chewed, the ends of noodles that stuck out of her mouth fell to her plate. Then she sucked the last string of noodle that remained and it flicked tomato sauce onto her cheek. Carla twisted a single noodle into her spoon and then inserted it carefully into her mouth. Bonnie picked up her knife and began cutting a noodle into tiny pieces before pushing a single piece onto her fork and eating it. They both laughed at this. Tom nudged a roasted artichoke onto his plate with a wooden spoon, then turned to Bonnie. Before he could dish her a share, Bonnie covered her plate with her hands.

"What is that?" she asked with her mouth full. A small piece of onion flew out as she did this and landed on her knuckles.

Tom looked away. "It's a vegetable."

"Why is it that colour?"

"Do we have a picky eater?" Tom said.

Bonnie seemed to consider this.

"Is that a rhetorical question?" Carla asked earnestly.

"Is that a rhetorical question?" The Douglas family laughed, but Bonnie did not laugh.

"What happened in school today?" Tom asked.

"Nothing," Carla said.

"Except ..." Bonnie prodded, elbowing his daughter in her side.

Carla looked up quickly, then darted her eyes down to her plate. "Shut up, Bonnie."

"Language," Tom stated.

Silverware clicked against the plates for a moment. "Well?" Tom said.

"Nothing—just that—"

Bonnie sucked her lips in, but the suspense was apparently too much for her to bear. "We had a food fight at lunch and Carla got baloney down her shirt!"

"Nothing stained anything—there was no mustard allowed. Mostly just raisins and nuts."

Tom raised his eyebrows, shook his head and returned to his artichoke. He hoped, for his daughter's sake, that there was more to success than a series of clever choices and hard work, that luck was also a possibility for some. "You've arrived, Tom," his mother used to say when she'd visit this house. And Tom would nod: the stone lions at the end of the driveway, the front door—made from old growth red cedar, knotless. The rewards of litigation, negotiation. It was a far cry from the duplex he grew up in, kids roaming the streets at all hours, daring each other to compare genitals or break car antennas. Then one day, that friend of Beverly's, the "investor"—that's the only description of his work he ever gave. "I used to be like you, Tom, trading hours for dollars. Selling your time gets you nowhere."

"It was really funny," Bonnie added, picking up a piece of chorizo and adding it to a pile on one side of her plate.

"Are you a vegetarian, Bonnie?" Tom asked.

"No." Carla and Bonnie looked at each other and laughed.

"What is so funny?"

"Bonnie ate the baloney that was in my shirt," Carla said, then grabbed her glass, shielding her smile.

Bonnie finished her noodles, but the pile of discarded sausage overshadowed this accomplishment like a compost heap on a freshly mowed lawn. Tom smiled gently, close lipped at first, but flashed his teeth before popping the sprig of basil into his mouth.

As Carla cleared the table for peach cobbler, Tom sat quietly. This made people nervous, and out of discomfort, they filled the silence by speaking first. It was a negotiation trick. He folded his serviette and placed it neatly in a rectangle on the right side of his plate.

Bonnie nodded.

Tom laced his hands together and leaned into them, elbows on the table. He breathed audibly through his nostrils as if he were sniffing his skin, held it there momentarily, then exhaled.

Bonnie nodded again.

"So your mother is foraging for mushrooms?" he said finally.

"Yeah." Bonnie leaned back in her chair. She looked comfortable.

"Quite the entrepreneur."

"What?"

"Ta-da!" Carla sang, heralding the emergence of the peach cobbler, wearing quilted oven mitts with a pattern of swallows and bluebells. She fetched the three bone china plates with gold flake rims, and three dessert forks, each one engraved with a different flower on the handle. This was a family heirloom from Beverly's side.

"You know, Bonnie, Carla made this cobbler herself."

"Dad ..."

Carla retrieved vanilla ice cream from the kitchen, and spooned some onto Bonnie's plate with a mechanical scoop so it made a perfect dome shape, the bottom melting into the cobbler, carving creamy streams between the mountainous peach wedges.

"What's that giant igloo back there?" Bonnie asked.

"It's an Authentic Italian Brick Oven."

"Oh." As Bonnie shovelled cobbler into her mouth, tilting the plate as she did so, every so often Carla glanced at this voraciousness and smiled very slightly. Tom could see that Bonnie, for some reason, was admired.

"It looks like an igloo," Bonnie said.

"So you say."

"Or like a big witch-wart." Bonnie seemed to ponder this further, puckering her lips and squinting, not in a way that made her look thoughtful, but suspicious. "Actually it looks like a stupa." With only a puddle of vanilla ice cream on her plate, Bonnie lifted it off the table to her mouth, like a cup, and slurped. Cream dribbled down her chin and onto her T-shirt and the tablecloth.

"You're stupa!" Carla said.

This made Bonnie laugh, but in an attempt to keep her mouth closed, the cream inside came out of her nose. Such a hilarious turn of events made it impossible for her not to turn pink with laughter, squealing. Carla cupped her mouth to conceal her own snorting.

Tom slammed his palm on the table, rattling the fork he'd laid across his own plate.

Bonnie and Carla stopped laughing and stared blankly at his fist. After a pause, Carla asked, "Are you all done, Bonnie?"

"Uh-huh." Bonnie followed Carla, carrying her own plate like a dog with its slobbery bone.

Tom glanced at the oven outside, then back to the table: soggy peaches in pools of melted cream, tomato-stained serviettes and bits of noodle stuck to the tablecloth. It looked like a picnic table havocked by gulls. After a few minutes, Carla came downstairs and asked timidly if he wanted them to do the dishes. Tom told her, no, but if she and Bonnie were going to behave like wild animals, they should take it outside. Carla and Bonnie put their shoes on.

Tom cleared the remaining dishes, loaded the dishwasher, and took the pork shank out of the fridge to rinse it in the sink, smoothing his palm over the peachy skin. He placed it on the wooden cutting board and daubed away moisture and droplets of congealed blood with a paper towel. He massaged olive oil into the roast, and followed with rock salt and rosemary, then placed it on a rack, put the rack in a roasting pan, and stowed it in the fridge for the night. Tomorrow was the day he christened the brick oven.

He went outside to take the temperature again. He was very impressed with how it retained heat. The dome was finally cooling, so the ash-coloured bricks inside were turning black again, the colour creeping up like a shadow from the sides of the dome. He unbuttoned his cuffs, rolled up his sleeves, and retrieved his buckskin work gloves from his workshop, the shed at the rear of the backyard. It was a miniature version of the house, complete with matching facia and wooden shutters, and the way it was tucked in behind the trees, it almost looked like a faraway cabin in the woods, but tidier, so that it had a dollhouse quality to it. Along its side was the wood Tom had purchased for the oven. One at a time, he carried the logs to stack them on the steel stand beneath the oven.

He had ensured the wood was free of any chemicals and selected a species with relatively little sap. The manual instructed him
to use clean burning wood, and never any fire starter, although he
could use a butane torch if he wanted, but this reminded him too
much of the barbeques of his childhood, with excessively tall flames
and too much fuel, sometimes fire crackers. Beverly wanted him to
return the oven immediately.

"You're overcompensating," she said. "You're trying too hard—
it's embarrassing." But now he wasn't so sure it was the stone lions
or the oven or any of that. It was something much more basic. After
the PTA meeting, he'd come home and lain on the bed without even
taking his shoes off.

"How was the meeting," Beverly had said to the dark.

"Long."

"I can smell you from here."

Beverly disapproved of marijuana unless she herself was smoking some. She was such a hypocrite. So Tom got up to wash the
sticky, ripe scent of pot away, dropping his clothes in the hamper.
But maybe that wasn't what she had meant.

He retrieved the broom which was leaning against the side of
the house. "Why is this here?" he said, annoyed with Carla, who
was supposed to sweep the patio. Didn't he tell her to do that? He
began sweeping up the chips of bark and dirt left from moving the
logs. Sweep: now it's gone. Sweep: now it's gone. The more he concentrated on this disappearing act, the more the patio seemed to
bulge up with each sweep, as if the weight of wood detritus was the
only thing holding it down. Tom was tired—stress, maybe. Dory. So
all this for one fleeting moment, an impulse—he was almost grateful to discover he still had those. It was just like Beverly to lord it
over him, unspoken barriers. She couldn't help herself—she grew
up that way. She probably just thought of him as a pig now, or some
dog smiling dopily with a bright red erection, unable to control its
actions, and incapable of explaining them. "Fuck Beverly," he said

aloud. He would like to fuck her right up against the side of the house, just like he did to Dory, and say, "This is what you're so mad about?" He would like to cum before she could even respond, just to make his point. Quick. Fleeting. Over.

"Get over yourself, Beverly," he said, and walked toward the workshop to empty the dust pan in the black compost bin behind. But the bin was no longer there. "What the fuck?" But Carla couldn't have moved the compost. His stomach fluttered, then felt extraordinarily heavy, and he wondered if the chorizo was past the date. When did he buy that chorizo? The sun suddenly retreated and the backyard took on a muted, monochromatic veil, the kind of light that flattens things, while at the same time accentuates texture, so the trees looked like photographs hung from the clouds. "Is it so late already?" Tom thought. When he looked back to the workshop, there was the compost bin. He must have had a floater in his eye. Maybe he had a migraine coming on. He dumped the pan and went into the workshop to whittle a perch.

Stupid little houses.

"I know that's what you think, Beverly." Tom rubbed his forehead. "But what do you do that's so important?"

Just not built to last.

Tom consulted his sketch book, flipped to the beginning—the dimensions of this first birdhouse. A quarter-inch diameter perch. "Speak for yourself," he said, rubbing his forehead. He grabbed the half a joint from the plastic soap container in the corner. He imagined Beverly in the doorway, arms crossed, smug.

This could all burn and we wouldn't have lost a thing.

Outside, a starling whistled. "You burn," he said.

~

When Tom woke, he was still in the workshop, slouched in the reclining chair with the water wheel patterned upholstery. He'd put the chair in there "for pondering." It was dark, so he couldn't see the clock above the door. Strange that he didn't have the light on. He moved his hands along the work table, toward the door. There was a little stick—a perch, perfectly planed and sanded by the feel of it. Did he make this? Yes, he must have. Yes, he smoked a joint, worked on this perch, then sat down for a moment, all before dark, all before switching the light on. Maybe he switched the light off—he had planned on sleeping here, perhaps. An impulse. Thump.

Carla's dormer window was dark. The girls must be in bed now, unless they're up watching TV. After all, what was the time? It could be ten. It could be three in the morning. Tom leaned against the outside of the workshop, still waking up. It smelled good, the minty-sour scent of fir, the acidic soil, years of needles piling up on each other. There was almost no grass in this yard for the acidity, just soil, compacted over heavy roots that clawed deeper and deeper into the ground each year, immoveable. These trees could never fall down, never. Tom imagined his house growing roots down below, unexpected, the way the eyes of a potato grow and grow even when they're forgotten in a dark trunk. Then he heard a voice.

"Shhh," it whispered.

There was nothing moving back here. The forest was a wash of blacks and greys, and as he tried to focus on shapes, they eluded him even more. The only thing he could clearly see was the fiery mouth of the oven, but wouldn't the wood have burned by now? But there it was, a red halfmoon, turned on its side. An eye. It wanted more wood. "More," it seemed to say.

"This is the oven talking," the voice whispered, but it seemed to come from behind him, in stereo, so that Tom wondered if he was hearing things. Was this a prank? The same person who tore the perch out of his house?

"Who's there?" he said. Maybe it wasn't Beverly after all.

"Feeeed me," it whispered again.

"Okay, I'll bite," Tom said. "What would you like to eat?"

Tom moved his weight from one foot to the other, leaning left and right, trying to find the voice. He stepped toward it, but timidly, unsure of the ground beneath.

"What would you like to eat?" he said again, louder this time. "I've got a lot of mouths to feed, so spit it out." He stepped again. A dog barked a few times far away. "What?"

A pause. A crack in the woods.

Then suddenly close, "YOU!"

A flurry of sound, pounding, crackling, like a startled grouse exploding out of the brush.

Tom clasped his chest, shouting after the intruder. "It's you who's gonna burn, you little shit!" Tom tried to run toward the sound, but he could only take one timid step at a time, his arms winging in front of him, beating the dark.

∾

Carla and Bonnie were already downstairs making a racket in the kitchen when Tom woke.

"I'm making pancakes, Dad. You want blueberries in yours?"

Carla wore her blue bathrobe with the yellow chick embroidered on the pocket. Her hair was in two braids and her bangs were held back with a pink hairband. She looked very grown up in a strange way. When Tom was a kid, he never saw any child with a bathrobe. Bonnie wore black sweatpants with elastic in the hems of the legs and a loose T-shirt. She was at the age when she really should start wearing a bra. But her mother didn't even wear a bra.

"Yes, sure, blueberries. Thank you, Carla." He glanced at the microwave: it was eleven o'clock already. "I slept like a log," he said.

"Us, too," Carla said, smiling at Bonnie, who sat on the other side of the counter.

"What does that mean?" Tom said, retrieving a coffee. He had the machine programmed to do it automatically at seven. It was already hours old, but he needed a coffee now. His head still ached.

"What do you mean, 'What does that mean?'" Carla eyeballed a pile of frozen blueberries into the mixing bowl.

"Never mind." Tom didn't care. They probably talked about sex or ate the rest of the cobbler or something.

"Bonnie's mom is coming to get her today, instead."

"What? Why?"

"She said she got her period and didn't want to have cramps when she was camping," Bonnie said.

Carla giggled. "I can't believe you told him that!"

"It's just bodies."

"What time?" Tom said.

"What time did she get her period?" Bonnie asked.

"No." Tom placed his coffee cup on the counter, turning it around, then around again. "When is she picking you up?"

Bonnie shrugged and picked at her pancake, popping a syrupy morsel into her mouth. "Afternoon. She wants to do errands first."

Tom needed to heat the brick oven to 600 Fahrenheit, allow the wood to burn down, remove the wood, roast the pork shank for a few hours. So he'd need to get it in there by about two. People were arriving around four. And Beverly was coming before that. She wanted to talk to him before the "charade." Three? He could phone her, ask her not to come early.

"I need you to call your mother and find out exactly what time."

"She won't be home," Bonnie said. "She was just leaving when she called here."

"For chrissakes."

"Dad?" Carla stopped mixing.

"Never mind, Carla," Tom took his coffee into the den.

"Do you still want a pancake?" Carla called.

Tom scrolled through the caller IDs on the phone, searching for the number to Beverly's parents' house, where she was staying. She had called Monday to tell him where she would be if anything important came up, and to explain to Carla what was happening, a story about needing to help her parents do an inventory of their belongings for legal purposes.

"Just leave it on the counter!" he called to Carla.

The phone rang three times without an answer. He slammed it down, assuming she had screened his call. Then the phone rang at his end. He picked up.

It was Beverly. "What do you want, Tom?"

"You called me," he said, picking up a pen and tapping it on the desk.

"I called you back."

Tom doodled on the page in front of him: a square, a triangle, a rectangle on top, a house with a chimney.

"Is that oven gone?" Beverly said.

A tree, a house in the tree. "What time are you coming?"

Beverly sighed on the line.

A man in the house, smoke.

"Why don't you just cancel this stupid party, Tom? I don't know what it is you intend to accomplish."

"Why don't you just come at four, like everybody else?" Four is not afternoon, is it? More like early evening.

"Honestly, I don't want to come at all. But I don't really have a choice. It's so tacky of you to have involved my friends in our marital problems."

Carla entered the room, holding a plate of two blueberry pancakes, garnished with cut strawberries. "Presenting ... My latest masterpiece!"

Tom snapped his fingers as he pointed to the door, mouthing "Go." Carla turned around, but not before Tom registered the disappointment on her face, her eyebrows knotted up in worry.

"This is such a waste of time," Beverly said. "I'll see you in a couple of hours." She hung up.

Tom pinched the bridge of his nose and massaged. His head was pounding now and his gut felt raw, as if he were developing an ulcer. He would have a glass of milk if it was still good. He can't

remember the last time he bought milk. Beverly usually did the grocery shopping. How long did milk last?

When Tom returned to the kitchen, Bonnie and Carla were
gone, leaving the drops of pancake batter to harden on the counter,
and a pile of plates varnished in syrup. How many plates do two
children need? He would have gone upstairs to tell her to finish the
job, but a feeling of guilt had sliced through the fog. She could be a
child of a broken home soon, which would be Beverly's doing. But
if the marriage broke down the middle, the house would, too. The
assets would be liquidated.

"I don't need your money, Tom," Beverly had said once. "I
just need you." This was supposed to be kind, soft words from soft
lips, but Tom just saw her sharp jaw chewing up his achievements
like tiny snacks, crumbs he'd only dropped on his way to success,
this place in the woods, his little, tiny, insignificant fucking yard
around his insignificant fucking house.

"Fuck you, Beverly," he said, as he imagined biting back. He'd
tear her to shreds. He'd feed her to the lions.

"Carla!" he shouted. "Get down here now!" He went to the
bottom of the stairs, called up again.

"Carla!" He could hear them whispering in her room, then the door
clicked open. "Get your ass down here now and clean up your mess."

Carla whispered something behind her, then said sheepishly,
"Should Bonnie help?"

"I don't care," Tom said. "I'm going out."

Tom thought he'd go to the grocery store and buy some milk,
then pick up another bottle of wine. He'd already purchased a few
whites in preparation, but an extra bottle wouldn't hurt. But the
sun was so bright, and the way it stabbed through the lacey patterns
of needles above hurt his eyes. He held one hand over them, the
insides of his lids glowing in reds and oranges and yellows. Maybe
he should just stay indoors.

He walked around to the backyard. The oven. He needed to

put wood in the oven. Fire it up. Six hundred Fahrenheit. What was he thinking, going to the grocery store? No. Too much to do here.

He placed the wood inside the oven. His arm was almost the same colour as the dome. Tom waited a moment before taking his hand out, noting the similarities: the faint lines where the stain settled unevenly, like blood vessels flushed beneath its skin. He imagined the oven's mouth closing tight around his wrist, like an anemone, slow suction, but then teeth, and he snapped his hand away. The sun was peering over the roof now, reflecting off the dome. Too fucking bright. Tom nursed the fire to life through squinted eyes before retreating to his workshop.

There was the perch, and a blue plate with the roach from last night's joint. He had more marijuana in the cookie tin on the top shelf. The tin once contained Christmas shortbread. "Who the fuck eats fucking shortbread?" he said, taking it down. He grabbed the wooden cutting board and sat in his chair with the board over his lap, scissoring a bud. But the greasy texture bothered him now. He should get one of those little metal things, those flat tins with teeth inside that twist and chew up the bud.

I'm gonna tear you up.

"I'm gonna tear you up, Beverly! You just watch. Nothing's gonna get past me."

He sucked deeply on the joint until it stabbed at his lungs, held it there, my prisoner. Exhaled. Smoked again, then leaned his head back, staring at the ceiling. Even the workshop was art—look at that joinery work. Closed his eyes, opened them. Every time he closed them, this compulsion to open again, yank up the blinds, make sure everything was still where he'd left it. There is the ceiling, there is the dark, there is the ceiling, there is the dark ... He placed the cutting board on the floor, leaned over to grab the perch, turning it around and around in his fingers. Had to get this perch up.

Then voices outside: "A stupa is a real thing. It's this thing you walk around and make wishes."

Stupid kid.

"Or people used to bury things in them, or burn things like presents to give dead people."

Then Carla: "Well, this is an Authentic Italian Brick Oven."

"I'm not saying it's not an oven—God! Who cares?"

Maybe Tom could just stay in here when Dory arrived. She wouldn't come looking for him—she had no sense of polite deport- ment. She would just take her kid and get out of here, and Tom wouldn't have to worry about anything. Or, if Beverly was here, they could go somewhere to talk—a café—they would have time. She was coming at one, an hour before the pork shank goes in.

"You always are the boss, and I have to be your sidekick." The girls were fighting now. Inevitable.

A sliding door slammed, and Bonnie shouted, "Carla!" The door opened again. Fainter, "Carla?!" Then quiet. He finished the joint, and added the roach to the pile on the blue plate.

The broken birdhouse was deeper in the trees, so Tom was protected from the glare of the sun. He leaned the aluminum exten- sion ladder against the tree, which fit safely; the tree was narrow enough that the ladder hugged each side. He placed the perch, the wood glue and the hammer in his tool belt.

One step at a time. The cold aluminum felt good in his hands. Tom touched his forehead to a rung, rocked his head to feel the cool across his brow. Another step. This was one of the first birdhouses he'd made. He'd never noticed anything in there before, which he thought was the result of too large an opening. He'd placed it fairly high on the tree, thinking a woodpecker might use it, but this nev- er happened. Still, he liked the look of it: Tudor, white with dark brown trim making triangles on the exterior. Another step. It was nice to go slow. He felt a little shaky—not nerves, just a good stone. What was the hurry, anyway? This tree would be here forever. So would Tom. Another step. Voices again. Little girl voices, lilting, then downward strokes, abrasive, really. They were sitting at the patio table, cutting some printer paper in half. Were those Tom's office scissors? Carla knew better than that. What were they discussing? The moment he thought it, he realized he didn't care. What did this mean?

Another step. He hadn't been paying attention to the trees back here. As he moved up the ladder, the trees appeared smaller, just overgrown ornaments, but ones that looked forgotten, left out in the rain, sagging branches and worn-out soil below. He surveyed his yard and spotted a patch of English ivy along the fence in the far corner. An invasive species. "You," he said, nodding. Now he would have to tear that out all the time. If left alone, it would take over the firs and cedars, twist around them, strangle them like a jungle snake, an English jungle snake, delicate as the plates with the gold flake trim, but deadly, hungry, going to swallow him whole, swallow these trees. Another step. Another step. Another step.

He reached the house. There was the perch. It was there.

Voices again. Tom turned. Girls circling the oven, holding papers. Bonnie twirled, then lost her balance, touched the ground with her hands, hopped once like a frog, up again. Carla twirled, balanced. Around and around, they carouselled the dome. Carouselled, careless, corralled. Pigs in a sty. Blow your house down.

He turned to the birdhouse and pinched the perch. "Pinch the perch," he laughed. Attempted to wiggle it, but it didn't move. "It is built to last," he said. Then, from inside the Tudor box, a faint but steady cheep, electronic almost in the way it punctuated time, a metronome heartbeat, *beat, beat, cheep, cheep*. So something had moved in. He almost turned to the girls, called, "Girls! Look at this!" But the impulse died the moment he thought of it. He wanted to keep this for himself—keep their paws off.

He tried to put his eye to the opening, but the way the roof extended past the side, and with that perch there, it was too awkward. Even if he had managed to put his eye to the hole, his own head would block any light and he wouldn't be able to see a thing.

"What are you doing, Dad?"

"Nothing."

"Are there babies inside?" Bonnie asked.

Go away. "I don't know."

Another step. He was slightly above the house now. He could lift off the roof, which was never nailed down, rest it on the top rung, and have a look inside. A nest of crow feathers, orange waxy needles and yellow grass cluttered the base of the box, and four grey chicks reached blindly up to him, wide bills gaping like yellow-lipped clowns. Pink bodies dusted with smoky down.

"Can I see?" Carla called.

Tom had seen these before. Greedy mouths, hungry for what-ever its oil-slicked parents could steal. Then they were foraging right now. They would return, shrieking and whistling, stuffing dead things into these ugly faces. Starlings.

"It was you!" Tom reached in and grabbed two—softly—he didn't want to crush them in his hand, their fine bones and guts snapping and oozing between his fingers, or throw them to the ground. He had another idea, but it was hard to carry them. He still felt shaky. He reminded himself to be loose with his grip, but then he felt as though he would drop them. He rushed down the ladder.

Carla hopped in one place, clapping her hands in time, and chanting, "We're gonna see the babies! We're gonna see the babies!"

But as Tom reached the bottom of the ladder, he pushed past the girls toward the patio. The yard dissolved and all he saw were the chicks on the cement in front of him. He pulled the hammer from the loop in his tool belt, squatting. He thought of them as rotten tomatoes. This could make a mess, but nothing a little soapy water couldn't clean up. But as he raised the hammer above him, a pair of arms constricted around his elbow, yanking him backwards and tweaking his shoulder, while Carla shouted something nearby. Carla rushed to the patio, kneeling by the chicks, trying to scoop them into her shaking hands. Tom had lost his balance and fallen back, so he was sitting down now. Bonnie had one hand on his hammer, the other trying to tear his fingers away one at a time. It was all so clumsy. It was slapstick, the way she clenched her teeth with the effort, her mane sweaty in the sun.

Tom let go of the hammer and Bonnie tumbled back, landing on her ass. "Whoopsy-daisy!" he laughed. He got up to take the birds from Carla, but stumbled, knocking her. The birds fell to the ground. "They're just starlings!" he said, scooping them up. Weeds. Maybe he should compost them. "You don't want the trees to die, do you?" No meat in the compost. He turned toward the oven. Clean burning, at least. He tossed the chicks inside.

He surveyed what was left. The table still needed to be win-dexed. "Carla," he said, pointing at the table. But Carla was on her hands and knees in the dirt, sobbing.

"Why did you that, Daddy?!" Bonnie walked over to her on all fours, placing one dusty hand around his daughter's shoulder. Carla continued to sob, saying, "Why did you do that? Why did you do that?" drool and mucus dripping out of her.

Why did you do that, Tom?

Tom shook his head. "They were starlings, I said." He looked inside the dome. Not a sound except for the soft popping here and there as moisture left the wood. The inside of the dome was peach again. This meant it was hot.

"Hello?" a woman called. Dory came around the side of the house, faded jeans and her hair up in a pile on the top of her head. "I tried knocking ..."

She wore a loose white blouse with a dark blazer. No, she didn't look as Tom remembered. This woman had a calculated style, a measured amount of carefree, tidily contained by this blazer. There was something designer about the fade in her jeans. Maybe she wasn't the welfare mom he'd imagined. Maybe she was loaded—stinking rich, just casual. Like a Hollywood actor. Good enough to eat, he almost said.

But she spotted the girls quickly and rushed across the patio, saying, "What's going on here? It's okay, Carla—what is it?" She smoothed his daughter's hair back, turning Carla's hands over, as if checking for injury. This only made Carla cry harder, like she had to push some trauma out. Why was she still crying?

"It's better for the other birds," Tom said. "Don't you care about the woodpeckers?"

But Carla continued to cry, sinking lower until she had her face against the backs of her hands, as if in supplication.

"What the hell happened here?" Dory said, keeping one hand on Carla's back. Bonnie handed her mother the hammer.

"Do I need to call the police?"

"He killed birds," Bonnie said.

Dory stared at the hammer, mouth gaping.

"In the oven," Bonnie pointed. "I saved them from the hammer."

What time was it now?

"Starlings," Tom stated.

Beverly was coming at one. The pork shank would go in at two. At three, something else would happen and this would be hours behind them.

"It was an impulse," Tom said. Thump.

You're done, Tom. You're done.

"You mean I'm cooked," Tom laughed.

"What?" Dory said.

But Tom had already turned away, and was wandering along the side of his house, up the cobblestoned walkway, past the impatiens and geraniums, to the driveway, up the driveway toward the stone lions, silent sentries. It would take decades of rain to wear these down. Yes, long after his daughter forgets all this, after Beverly forgets it, too, these statues would be here.

71

Art

The children were fussy. When the temperature dipped below minus twenty-five, the only time they left the daycare was to be walked to or from kindergarten. This week, there was a cold snap. But Linda did her best to keep the children engaged, despite her co-worker, Rhonda, who considered enthusiasm merely a symptom of inexperience. That morning, she had completed her application to the Education program at the university. If they gave her credit for the courses she took in the nineties it would only take two and a half years to finish her degree, which was probably all she could afford. She didn't want to erode her retirement savings. Sometimes this university even gave credit for "related work experience," which is one of the reasons Linda wanted this job. She'd had to write an essay explaining this. So who knows, maybe she would be the kindergarten teacher one day, see Rhonda at the playground, then blow her whistle for all her students to line up, eager to go in for whatever afternoon craft Linda has planned.

Linda stapled the head of a purple centipede on the wall in the dramatic play area. There were ten pieces to this centipede. Linda had made it herself, laminating each section with clear packing tape. Rhonda sat at the art table, picking her cuticles, where the five-year old-girls traced cookie cutters on scrap paper.

They'd been co-teachers at the daycare for six snowy months. Every week, Linda retrieved new books from the basement for circle time, selected new songs and learned their respective chords on the guitar with the missing string. She had painted flowers on the circle time window one week before.

"Flowers in the middle of winter?" Rhonda had criticized. Exactly, thought Linda. It was bleak outside. Maybe Linda would mention the Education degree program today. Rhonda would raise her eyebrows at that, surely.

"Dustin, get out of the sand table!" Rhonda shouted without getting up. Linda stapled the last of the centipede and stepped back to admire the way its body went up and down, suggesting movement over uneven terrain.

"Why?" Dustin said, slapping his sandy palms together over the table, a plastic tub on a four-legged aluminum frame.

"You got sand in my eyes!" another boy whined.

Rhonda stood up and pushed her fists into her waist. "Dustin Percival Smythe, you watch your step or I will have to take some serious action here."

More threats, thought Linda, and stuffed a few plush toys onto the shelf—a ladybug, a witch, a lion. The lion had little to do with the *James and the Giant Peach* theme, but they were out of bugs and witches. There was another old lady doll with dimpled cheeks and chin, but she had only a week ago served as the protagonist for Gramma's house.

"You can't expect the children to have tea with her one week and make her cast spells the next," Rhonda had complained.

"You can play in here, Dustin," Linda said. Dustin looked at the purple centipede and thumped toward the area, groaning.

Rhonda lunged one foot forward and grabbed Dustin's sleeve. "No. Water table. Go." She steered Dustin's shoulders to the tub of water dyed with orange food colouring and filled with cups, plastic zoo animals and boats, then returned to the dramatic play area and examined the centipede, pursing her lips and squinting. "The water table calms a child, not the dramatic play area," she said finally and kneeled down to reorganize the shelf of toys.

Rhonda scratched her head. Her pink fingernails scraped at grey roots, which were followed by a section of carrot orange, then dark auburn. Rhonda's hair looked terrible. It was probably bad for staff morale, even, a sort of depressing forecast of their futures if they worked here too long. But Rhonda still doled out advice.

"What have you got on today, Linda?" she'd said once. "There's no reason for someone our age to look that frumpy!" Linda had been wearing a hooded sweater and jeans. Rhonda was in a knee-length sweater and spandex. Besides that, Rhonda was ten or fifteen years older than Linda, wasn't she?

Linda put down the stapler and wandered toward the sink, twisting the ring on her finger. It was silver, stained black in the grooves where the tiny gecko anchored its metal feet. On the inside it said Made in Mexico. It gave her an eclectic look, although she'd never been to Mexico. She imagined travelling there one day, walking along beaches in a cotton wrap and discovering secluded spots hidden by towering cacti, or broad-leafed tropical plants, maybe. She thought of Montezuma, Cortés, Pancho Villa. She'd taken a Latin American studies class once, although the focus was primarily on the twentieth century, politics and revolution. If she gets into this program, she would like to learn more about that culture, maybe take a Spanish language class. This could help her in her field. She'd teach the children about multiculturalism, make new immigrant families feel welcome. Maybe she should have written something about this in her application.

She bent over the sink to drink from the tap. If Rhonda was watching, she would have told her to use the paper cups, that she's setting a bad example. Linda looked sideways at the room: round carpet, art table, sand table, dramatic play area canopied with the sheet Linda had tie-dyed orange over the weekend to look like the outside of the peach. She closed her eyes, not really drinking anymore and let the water trickle over her mouth, then *smack, smack, smack* on the bottom of the sink. One by one, the sounds of the room filtered past the water: low drone of central heating, feet thumping on carpet, scuffing across linoleum, wooden blocks knocking, lilting voices of girls playing house, punchy sounds of boys rallying round their leader, a pencil grinding in the sharpener. Linda opened her eyes. The snow outside reflected on the windows, blinding her and the colours of children's clothes blurred like wildflowers in an allergic haze.

John, the teary boy at the sand table, came into focus, his white-blonde head barely discernible from the snow-blind windows behind. Linda squatted down beside him and shovelled sand into a blue dump truck. He was still rubbing his eyes when Linda started to help build the mountain.

His hands jumped back into the table. "It needs more sand over here, on this side, because it has to be even to make it a volcano."

Linda smiled. "Why does a volcano need to be even?"

John shrugged. "Because."

Linda made a gargling sound as she pushed the blue truck around to the other side of the sand pile. If she was going to learn Spanish, she would have to learn how to roll her R's. Rhonda was still in the dramatic play area, assessing it like a pigeon approaching a piece of garbage. It was February and she was still wearing that fleece Christmas sweater with the green felt sock and glue-gunned yarn announcing, "Happy Xmas." It might have been funny, but they'd been caged in this room together for too long. Linda hadn't even bothered to ask Rhonda for a reference on her application. She put the daycare director's name instead, who was just impressed that Linda spent her own money on art supplies sometimes.

"It's all uneven!" John said, looking to the side of the volcano where Linda had just dumped her pile of sand.

"It's alright, John, we can even it out—"

John barricaded the volcano with his hands. "No!"

"Okay, okay," she said, "I'll let you do it." John snatched pinch-fuls of sand from Linda's pile, then sprinkled them on the volcano.

If John wasn't so fussy, she could have taught him how volcanoes were made, something about magma and the centre of the earth. Maybe this summer she could turn the dramatic play area into a geologist's lab, find storybooks about Hawaii, get a ukulele. She'd seen a blue one for sale at the guitar store—only twenty dollars. "Who's gonna teach them?" Rhonda would say. Linda would. She'd buy a chord chart and learn a few chords. It was close enough to guitar, so she could probably lead circle time with it. The kids could take turns plucking a string, learn how to treat it gently. They wouldn't even care if it was out of tune—they weren't judgmental like the adult world. She'd seen the way some parents turned their noses up at the room. Like the Chinese New Year dragon Linda had made with the strip of a bed sheet and decorated with flowers made from coloured tissue paper.

"Did the kids make that today?" one mother asked. The kids— she really thought five-year-olds were capable of detailing scales and constructing this three-dimensional head?

"No, I did," Linda had said.

"Oh." The woman smiled, not in a way that made her look pleased, but embarrassed.

Another parent even asked flat out why Linda did not "include the children in the project." She just wanted her classroom to look nice and she did so much for them, didn't she? It was the children who appreciated Linda's time and Linda's love.

She left John to his fussy volcano and wandered to the art table. A few of the girls sat together at one end, quietly drawing with pencils. "I like the way you're sharing those pencils," she said to them.

Kaitlin sat at the other end of the table, cutting a purple sheet of paper.

Linda pulled out a tiny blue chair across from her. "How's it goin'?"

Kaitlin glanced up, then back to her paper. "Fine."

Linda sat down. She was tall, so the chairs made her feel gangly. She thought of the Popeye cartoons, Olive Oyl wagging her long boneless arms above her head. Linda looked at the floor. It was dirty, scarred with sand table legs, water table legs, corners of shelves, rubber soles shuffling across. Years of children's muddy sneakers, sticky hands, pizza grease and glue had stained it. Bits of dry playdough and sparkles collected along the baseboards. On the table were dried-up blobs of white glue. Linda picked at one that had fossilized enough dust to turn it matte grey.

Kaitlin scrunched her nose. "That's gross."

"It's just glue," Linda said. Maybe Kaitlin needs to know it's okay to get her hands dirty.

The scissors made a growling sound as they cut off triangles. "So?"

Kaitlin seemed a little defensive. She often played alone. Linda had noted this in the classroom observation book when she first started working here, until Rhonda told her she should wait until she actually knows the kids before she goes and makes mountains out of mole hills. But Rhonda never wrote anything down. At least Linda cared. But after that, she wasn't really sure what to write. Should she make a note about John's volcano?

"Did you know purple is a royal colour?" Kaitlin said. "Purple and gold."

"Oh?"

"My bedroom is pink but I'm changing it to one of those colours."

"Change is good," said Linda. Kids shouldn't fear change. That can really hold a person back. That can get a person really stuck. You have to throw caution to the wind sometimes, have faith in yourself. She would have told her about the university application, but Kaitlin was too young to understand anything about that. "Gonna paint or something?"

"Yes," Kaitlin said. "And I'm getting new sheets and a lamp to match."

"Sounds pretty fancy-shmancy."

"It's not even fancy," Kaitlin corrected. "Fancy would be if I had a canopy bed, too, but my dad said that would be excessive." Kaitlin stopped cutting to pronounce the word, jutting her chin forward, then looked at Linda, who only nodded.

"Not excellent, excessive," Kaitlin said.

Linda nodded again, "Yes, I know."

"Okay, because a lot of people don't know that word. I only know it because my dad is a professor. That's not a teacher, teachers are lower."

Linda stopped picking at the glue.

Kaitlin snipped the last of the purple sheet into triangles. She put down her scissors and flipped through the basket of construction paper in the centre of the table until she pulled out a yellow sheet. "This isn't gold but it will have to do, I guess."

The stapler crunched against the wall behind. Rhonda was restapling the purple centipede. Linda took a red sheet of paper and a pair of tiny scissors from the basket and snipped off a corner.

"You know, Kaitlin," she said, "teachers have to go to university, too. They go to school for a long time."

Kaitlin continued cutting without looking up.

"They need a degree and then they have to go to school even more to learn about teaching." Linda remembered the list of prerequisites the academic advisor had printed out for her when she'd first started university. But an Education degree was expensive and there were no guarantees. She would probably have to live in some remote town just to get her foot in the door and she had a life in the city—a cat, although he died a long time ago now; a girlfriend. And she'd just got hired as a casual office admin assistant for the health association, which would mean she could now apply for all the internal postings and the pay was decent—better than decent. It was a union job and she would just keep moving up the seniority list.

Kaitlin tilted her head from one side to the other, snipping perfect triangles. "What do you know, anyway?"

Linda cut a triangle from the corner of the red sheet. "What do I know?" she asked. What does a five-year-old know, she wanted to say, but instead asked what Kaitlin wanted to be when she grew up.

"I'm probably going to be an artist," she said.

"I can see you like art. You're always at the art table."

Kaitlin smiled and Linda felt jealous, but that was ridiculous, wasn't it? She should encourage this self-assuredness. If only Linda had been so lucky. She never felt talented when she was a kid. She avoided the bars in the playground; they were always swarmed with kids in gymnastics. She avoided the field on the off chance a ball was kicked in her direction and she'd be expected to send it back, a potential humiliation if she offered a lame kick, or just scuffed it clumsily. She stayed in the art room instead when she could, or just walked the perimeter of the school grounds as if she had somewhere to go. She daydreamed of being pulled aside, or called to the principal's office, sat down to discuss her hidden talent, this potential that must be unleashed and only could be with special attention. From now on, they would say, she would have one-on-one time with the teacher—we simply cannot let you go to waste. Maybe one day Linda could be that teacher to a child—unlock something, open a door for them. It could change their life.

Linda snipped another piece. Her long fingers fiddled awkwardly in the tiny handles and the piece fell on the table with four points instead of three. She cut another shape, this one with one rounded side. The next was a rhombus. She could tell Kaitlin that. Teach her some geometry. A mosaic of shapes. She thought of the collection of old plates, goblets and clay mugs she'd picked up from the thrift store last summer. She'd put them in a box, covered them with a towel, then smashed them with a hammer. Now the pieces were laid in mortar behind her kitchen sink, swirling down the wall like green, blue and purple waves.

Kaitlin stopped cutting to gape at the red polygons collecting in front of Linda.

"What are you doing?" she asked, her eyes wide.

"I'm helping. I'm cutting more shapes for your collage."

"I'm making a mosaic," Kaitlin corrected.

"That's so exciting! I've made mosaics before, you know. You might want to make use of my expertise." Linda held her hand daintily midair as she said this, as if the word were so old-fashioned. She was trying to be funny, but Kaitlin didn't laugh.

"I want it to be good," Kaitlin said. "It's for my dad. You can't help."

Rhonda walked toward the circle time area, poking Linda's shoulder on the way by, chortling like a pig. Linda let her hand fall to the table and leaned forward, confused. "Why not?"

"Because," Kaitlin said, leaning forward with her chin out, "You are a philistine." Kaitlin put down her scissors and repositioned a blue dragonfly barrette in her hair. "Why don't you just go away? Maybe you can help John or something."

Linda stared as Kaitlin rifled through the basket for another sheet of paper. With one hand she brushed away a few of Linda's red polygons that had drifted toward her triangles. Linda felt her hands sweat and wiped them on her jeans, then held them between her knees and squeezed. They were shaky. Behind her, John started to cry.

"He wrecked my volcano!" he said, pointing to Dustin, who was running on tiptoes toward the sink. "He wrecked my volcano!" John cried again. Dustin was casually taking a paper cup and filling it with water.

Rhonda looked up from the round carpet where she was now reinforcing book spines with packing tape. Linda sat at the table between Rhonda and the wailing child, still staring at Kaitlin.

"Dustin Percival Smythe!" Rhonda said, marching toward John. She held John's shoulders and spun him around, displaying the teary mess to Dustin. "Get over here now and apologize."

Dustin walked calmly over to the sand table. Rhonda crossed her arms, waiting for the apology, but instead, Dustin dumped his cup of water on what was left of the sand volcano. John howled, pinched Dustin's arm and twisted it. Dustin punched John, hitting him in the chest and ran out of the room.

"Linda!" Rhonda said, pointing at John, "You deal with this." She ran after Dustin, who was probably in the playroom by now, hiding in the foam blocks. Linda tried to think of what to say to Kaitlin. Should she write this down in the book? Should she talk to her father about it? The professor? Would he just survey the room, with that same muted smile? The dragon, the centipede, bed sheet art, Rhonda and her Xmas sweater, Linda's co-worker, her equal.

John gripped the edge of the sand table and stomped his feet, his ribcage convulsing with tears.

Kaitlin put down her scissors and rolled her eyes up at the ceiling. "What is that baby crying about, anyway," she said. "It's just a pile of sand."

Kaitlin walked over to the sand table where children were beginning to congregate, some staring at John and the soupy puddle of what once was a volcano, others waiting for Linda to get up and console their fallen comrade. But Linda was focused on staying seated, containing the anger that now burned in her chest.

Kaitlin leaned on the opposite side of the sand table, raised herself onto her toes and assessed the destruction. "That was a volcano?" She giggled and walked back to the art table. She leaned on her elbows, still standing but bent at the waist and began stacking her triangles into tidy piles. "He doesn't even know what a volcano is, probably."

The corners of Kaitlin's mouth rose smugly. Kaitlin's weight was on one foot now and she swung her hips back and forth. John's sobs continued to gurgle behind Linda, periodically hiccupping gulps of air.

"He's just a no-talent," Kaitlin proclaimed.

Linda lunged at Kaitlin, squeezed her arms. "Where do you get off?" she shouted, shaking her once so her eyes popped wide open, round as snowballs. "Who do you think you are?" Linda shook her until Kaitlin's blue dragonfly barrette came loose and hung from fine hairs down to her cheek.

Kaitlin squeezed her eyes shut, turning her head away. Linda pushed her, releasing her grip and Kaitlin tumbled backward, hit her head on the art shelf behind and fell to the ground. She lay on her side, curled up, crying and red in the snow-white light.

"What is all this screaming!" Rhonda shouted as she ran back into the room. She gathered Kaitlin into her fleecy chest, rocking her and smoothing back the fine hair, now wet with tears. "Who's responsible for this?" she demanded. "This is unbelievable, Linda. I leave the room for one second—"

Linda got up and walked out of the room. Rhonda called her again, then told the children to return to their play, insisting everything was fine.

Dustin was sitting in the cloakroom area, half swallowed up by coats and snow pants, chewing at a fingernail. "I'm not supposed to go anywhere," he said.

Linda looked at the window opposite them. The playground outside was empty. She imagined tongues freezing to swing set chains.

Reflection Journal

For my "reflection journal" I would like to say that this is stupid. First off, this is not really a journal if you're going to read it when I'm done, so the whole premise of this "reflection" is flawed. Second, Mr. Diaz is paranoid. Anyone who can teach a unit on Greek and Roman myth and then get upset when a student illustrates some of it deserves to be harassed. Now I will doodle.

I just drew a penis on the back of this page. That is probably very disturbing for you, or maybe you think it's some indication of latent Oedipal emotions, or Electra emotions, or whatever. You can't really say that, though, because you're just a counselor. Anyway, it's actually the beginning of a satyr. Those are the guys with huge erections that dance around in Greek tragedies. See? I do pay attention to something other than Mr. Diaz's buttoned-up shirts and khakis. He irons his jeans, too. I saw a crease down the legs once, unless it was just left-over from how he folds his pants. Maybe now I will draw the rest of the satyr, except I'll give him a guitar instead of a lyre since that's more realistic for modern times. I can't say anything about the accurateness of the erection, though. It may shock you to know that I've never seen an erect penis, since you think we're all on the verge of pregnancy and AIDS. And even if that were true, I'd rather take the bus to a walk-in clinic and talk to a white-haired doctor about setting up an abortion before I'd talk to a high school counselor. As if one of your pamphlets would make me care, anyway. But that won't be a concern for me, as I said. There's enough schoolyard discussion about hard-ons for me to infer the reality. Mr. Diaz would approve of that sentence, "infer the reality." He likes academic crap like that.

I'm watching the clock. It's five after three. Forty more minutes of reflecting. I think Mr. Diaz should also reflect on why he practically had an anxiety attack about my "behaviour." It was Valentine's Day, after all. This is when the Romans would have fertility celebrations, like whipping fields and women's butts. I stole a book about it. (I steal from Chapters all the time.) Mr. Diaz should have been impressed—how many other students would take such an enthusiastic interest in mythology? It was very time consuming to make that comic strip, too. You have to design the panels, decide on the storyboard before you draw it, pencil it in, ink it in, add colour. I thought my Juno comic was pretty funny, and the picture I only included because it was handy. Trina took it last week with this disposable camera we stole from the grocery store. Development is included, so it's really the cheapest way to steal a camera.

Nice smock, or whatever it is you're wearing. You look like some wannabe African choir director with all those orange zig-zags, except you're not African. Just some fat white lady with poofy hair. It's no wonder no one wants to spill their guts to you. And I can tell you're not actually reading. You're purposely ignoring me. A person can sense when they're being looked at even if you can't see it in your peripheral vision. You can feel people's eyes on you, like warm spots. I have to pee now, but you'll probably add the three minutes to my time here if I leave. Blah, blah, blah. I'm going to ask.

Apparently, you don't think I have a right to urinate. I've reflected on that and I think that is physical abuse. For me to delay urinating puts stress on my bladder, causing urinary tract infections down the road. If I get an infection, I will be sure to sue the school district. And this "reflection" is documentation of this incident. Hardcopy evidence is very important. That's why prenuptial contracts exist. You can't take anyone's word for anything.

It's very hypocritical that you ask personal questions about people and then tell them it's inappropriate when they do the same thing back. When you automatically believe everything Mr. Diaz tells you, and completely take his side, what do you expect me to think? He drags me in here and talks about me like I'm not even here, saying SHE gave me this inappropriate gift, SHE is trying to sabotage my career, if the roles were reversed this would be sexual harassment. You nod, watch his shaky hands and blue eyes like he was trying to burn a hole into you. "Calm down, Kenneth," you say, "it's okay," in your try-hard soother voice. Everyone knows your husband left you last year. You're probably lonely and desperate.

I just added a bottle of wine and some cups to my drawing, which I guess is transforming this into a sort of Dionysian festival. That's the guy with the beard and the drugged-up crazy women that follow him around and nurse pigs. They let piglets suck on their nipples and then sacrifice them. One guy sees his mother doing this stuff, then she sees him and kills him, thinking he's a lion. I think if he hadn't been killed, he probably would have wanted to poke his eyes out anyways, which is a whole other story.

I don't understand why Mr. Diaz didn't just tell me why he was so pissed off. If I had given him a Christmas card, I don't think any of this would be happening. A Valentine's comic strip seemed both relevant to the class content, and original and creative. It's not like it was a naked picture of me. I was wearing overalls and a T-shirt and blowing a kiss at the camera, which Trina was holding. People blow kisses to babies, the queen blows kisses to the English masses, or whoever is watching her roll by in her little pastel blazer suits. Actors at the end of plays—they accept flowers, too. Roses, even, but I'm sure if I'd given Mr. Diaz a rose, I would probably still end up here. Mr. Diaz and I were friends. He told me he was happy I was in his class and that it was "refreshing" to hear "such intellectual thinking." But you don't care about any of this stuff because I'm a "bad kid," stealing from Chapters and Save-on-Foods—but those are victimless crimes. It's the violent criminals you should be worried about. But then I guess Mr. Diaz is saying that he's a victim. A victim of too much attention? The only reason I phoned him was because I didn't know who else to talk to. Don't you encourage us to talk about our problems? I didn't want to go to you because everyone says you tell the other teachers even though it's supposed to be confidential, and you'd probably just focus on my stealing problem, or ask me stupid crap about my mother. If Mr. Diaz can talk about swans raping people, I don't see how he could have been upset about my comic.

Now you're pretending to organize your filing cabinet. Maybe you're trying to get some exercise.

I can see Trina outside on the portable steps right now talking to Andrew Chong. She told me yesterday she has the hots for him but I think he's totally conceited. And he's recently decided he's funny, and it seems like most people agree. But all he does is say, "bangers and mash!" randomly out of nowhere, and this always gets laughs. Even the Canadian Studies teacher laughed at this and I thought it was very disruptive. Plus, if she laughs at this, she's sending a message to the class that this kind of behaviour is okay from Andrew, but probably not anyone else. If I shouted something random like "garlic toast," or "sex on the beach," I doubt anyone would think I was so special. Mr. Diaz would probably stare Andrew down if he tried to be funny in his class, silence him with his eyes.

I can't figure out why my comic strip was so bad, but the other presents weren't. Like the CD. I got this CD of *My Fair Lady*—which is actually based on the play, *Pygmalion*, which is from the Greek myth about the guy who goes for the statue. It was right there on this discount table at the music store by that gross muffin place and no one was looking, so I took it and I gave it to Mr. Diaz. Obviously, I realize that *My Fair Lady* isn't really like *Pygmalion* and the statue, but it was free and I didn't want it because I don't listen to fairy-tale crap like that, so it was really no big deal to give it to Mr. Diaz. I didn't even think he'd want it, but I didn't really have anyone else to give it to—Trina isn't into that crap either. Right now she likes Beastie Boys, who are really obnoxious, but that's her type, as I said.

Anyways, Mr. Diaz said it was "thoughtful" and offered to treat me to a mocha, but he never suggested a time, so I figured he meant giving me a gift certificate or something, so I said "that's okay, just take it." Then he just said he had marking to do and I should go. Then I wondered if it was rude of me not to accept a gift card, but I don't think you should have to repay someone with a gift. The point of a gift is that it's just for the other person, just to be thoughtful and nice, and the CD was free, anyway. It probably isn't even worth a mocha. If I'd accepted a mocha, I would have been ripping him off. So I said I was sorry, and he said don't be sorry, you can't help it, you're a child. And that made me angry how he had changed me like that, so yes, maybe I was mad at him, and maybe my comic went a little overboard, but just to get a rise. When Andrew Chong yells out "bangers and mash!" that's obviously a cry for help but I don't see him in here reflecting on that. Why bangers and mash, anyway? It makes no sense.

Stupid lead. At least I was allowed to sharpen my pencil. I will state for the record that I did not break the tip on purpose, but it was good to get out of this chair. I'll probably have chronic back pain from sitting in these cheap chairs all day. When I'm thirty and my chiropractor bills start piling up, I'll sue the district. I'll be sure to record back pain in my private, legitimate journal when I get home.

It's almost 3:20. Time is going so slow.

Trina and Andrew are sharing headphones now. Now she's taking out her headphone and Andrew is saying something. Now she's laughing. Trina acts so stupid around Andrew. When it's just the two of us she's funny and gross—she likes talking about her shits and she's really good at special effects makeup. But as soon as Andrew appears, she puts her hands in her back pockets so her tits stick out and just laughs at his stupid jokes. Bangers and mash. I wonder if that's supposed to be sexual. The banger is shaped like a penis, plus the word "bang" in there, then the mash. The mash part doesn't really make sense but people compare the dumbest things to vaginas. Boxes, muffins, beavers. Beavers are the largest rodents in North America, and a vagina does not have teeth. Mr. Diaz is more respectful about that kind of thing. He brings slides in sometimes of paintings of myths like Venus on the clamshell, or Leda and the swan, which is actually Zeus and he's raping her—Zeus is the swan, I mean. This slide got a lot of laughs. The idea of a swan raping a woman is funny to people like Andrew and now Trina, too. Mr. Diaz turned off the projector and just looked at the class without speaking, until people were quiet and then he said that this is a place to learn and if you don't have the maturity to discuss this in a manner that is respectful to the young women in the room then you should leave now. Of course no one left. And he was right. When he passed my desk after the slide show, he touched my shoulder so I'd know that he knows I'm more mature than that. That I know there is nothing funny about a swan raping a girl. It's more disgusting than funny—more frightening than disgusting. A gigantic swan, splaying its webbed grey feet, heavy enough to hold you down and then what? Does it use its swan penis? What if it puts its entire head and neck inside, with the hard orange beak—and have you seen swans eat? They jab. And then she's pregnant, and she has the baby, who is Helen, who is apparently beautiful enough to start a war, or beautiful enough to be kidnapped and then the men start the war, as if war is that simple.

With all this raping and kidnapping, it's hard to believe Mr. Diaz could get so shaken up by me, a girl. I thought sexual harassment had to be when someone in a position of power harasses someone lower down. He used to let me hang out in the portable where he did his marking. I liked being there because it was quiet and no one around to look at you like at the library. You look up and people are between the stacks or sitting at tables or in carrels, and there's encyclopedias in front of them and spiral notebooks, and they're quiet but you can tell they're not studying. There's all these eyeball conversations going on and then someone laughs like a belch through the nose and you know that there is some joke, but you don't know who it's on. It could be on you, you don't know. It could be about your hair or maybe you stink or maybe your butt looks fat mushed against the chair—you don't know. So I liked Mr. Diaz's portable. And if he looked at me it was different because I knew it was respectful. I liked the sound of his pencil, too. He said he thought it was more respectful to mark that way. He said that using ink was too authoritative and he didn't put himself on a pedestal like that. One day, we stayed there doing our work together and talking until 5:30, when he said he had to go home because his girlfriend was over and she was making her "famous mango chicken." Then we laughed because it's too suburban for him. He's not a mango-chicken-with the-little-woman type of person. Then he said I could talk to him whenever I needed to, even on the weekend, and he gave me his phone number. But I already had it from the other time I called him, when I just looked up Mr. Diaz in the phone book—it's not like I had to be a detective to find it. But I said thanks and it was nice that he gave me the number that time because then I had a hardcopy for when I needed it. When I got home, there was no mango-chicken waiting for me (thank God), just the house because my dad is doing his millionth marathon and out training, as usual, not that I care. But I'm sure you'll read into that anyway. But that night was kind of strange because my mom phoned, which is weird. She phones maybe once every six months to talk to Dad and try and get some money. So instead she asks me for money, as if I could possibly have any, as if I would ever give her any even if I did have some, so I told her why don't you just go suck someone off or would that mean having to get off the couch. Then she started crying so I said piss and moan on your own time and hung up on her. But then I was mad, or something, so I phoned Trina, who just said "your mom is such a bitch," which she is, but I didn't want her to say that. She's my mother, and what is so fucking fantastic about Trina's mom? She looks like a mushy apple on two popsicle sticks and she's always giving me advice. She thinks a couple child psychology classes makes her an expert. A year of college and she's an academic. She's an idiot so I called Mr. Diaz. The mango-chicken-woman answered but wouldn't just give the phone to Mr. Diaz. She kept repeating "can I tell him who's calling, who shall I say is calling" until I finally had to give her my name and then Mr. Diaz took the phone and I told him about my mom wanting money and what Trina said and what an idiot her mother is, and he just said it's not appropriate to call me and how did you get my number, and then said I should talk to YOU. Then he told me to calm down because I was starting to cry, and mango-chicken said something but I didn't hear, and Mr. Diaz said to her "I don't know, I don't know." I asked him why he was doing this and he said I'm hanging up now, I'm hanging up now, and then he did.

Ever since that phone call things were different. So it's really me who is the victim. Not sexual harassment, but emotional abuse. First he is there, and then he's gone. He's just a teacher again, an up-tight, rigid teacher who irons his jeans. Well, if that's what he wants to be now, then I will just be a student. I will be the bad kid with the deadbeat mom who steals. Fine. So I made the comic, a funny comic strip about Juno, a hilarious role reversal, which you prob-ably didn't understand. But if Juno gets the Romans to whip the men on the ass for a change, then they should become more fertile, right? And what's a symbol of male virility? Erect penises. That's why the erect penises. And back then they thought of sex as a man ploughing a woman, like she's a field, so the erect penises plough the actual field instead and then Juno says, "Finally figured out what to do with those." Big deal. Big fucking deal. Ooooooh, boners, better call the cops. It wasn't an attack at Mr. Diaz, specifically. I'm sure his boners are good for other things, but you would have to ask mango-chicken about that. But with Zeus raping everyone, I think it is really, really, really hypocritical that my comic is getting such a reaction. So, okay, if the roles had been reversed, and Mr. Diaz had made a Juno comic strip for me, that would be bad because it would show favouritism. Everyone would know he thought I was special. Imagine if a teacher brings an apple to school to put on his favourite student's desk. But Mr. Diaz has brought things for the whole class, like the Leda and the Swan painting. It's not as if we need to see that painting to understand the story in the hand-out. Or the painting of Artemis in the bath, or the marble statues of Hades grabbing at Persephone, or Apollo trying to rape Daphne. We are literate (most of us). So this role reversal thing is not parallel. The class is a whole entity and the teacher is an entity. And I definitely wouldn't want some erect phallus in me, like a big swan beak jabbing at my mashed potatoes. Plus, Mr. Diaz is thirty-four. That is TWICE my age. If I were seriously sexually harassing him, that would make me a kind of reverse-pedophile, and I am just a thief. That is a whole other psychology from diddlers. Even prisoners know that. In jail, pedophiles get killed or raped, and thieves get seconds and thirds at dinner because we're crafty. We're smart. I'm an intelligent person with refreshing ideas, and that's why I have a harder time than everyone else. Mr. Diaz knew that. He said I know you're dealing with a lot of uncomfortable feelings, and yes, yes I was. He knew about my mom. And a marathon is forty-two kilometres and that takes a lot of work, and there never is anything to go home to, so he said I could stay with him if I needed to get away, that there's lots of room in the place because his girlfriend only stays there weekends. I could read or look at art, he said, and I said thank you that time, and I would like that. But I never did go over there and maybe that's why he was so upset about the Juno thing. Maybe he thinks it was all a joke to me. Maybe he thinks the CD was a joke and the phone call was a prank, that I just met up with Trina after all those things to laugh at stupid Mr. Diaz the way we laugh at you and your "reaching out" crap. That I never did look up to him, never did need his friendship or afternoons marking papers or touches on the shoulder. That I never wanted to be special.

Monsters

I used to be afraid of what was under my bed, until I looked. After that, I wanted to know who the bad people were.

I found out by accident. Mom simply misunderstood me. "I was talking about Vincent," I said.

"Jesus Christ, Mallory."

A few weeks before that, the child-killer Clifford Olson died, and it was on the news. I wondered about the bodies, where exactly they'd been found. I was a little kid when all that happened, and I always imagined they were somewhere near our old house, buried in a row at the back of my elementary school field, by the baseball diamond. I looked online: there was one in Richmond, two in Aggasiz; a local girl looking for work; a German traveller murdered with a hammer. But there were nine more. I could picture the scene like a TV crime drama, the school field barricaded with a white tent, men in bio-suits coming in and out, so I searched online for "Meadow Elementary + body found." I found Vincent. There he was, in a community news website, not as he would look today, a man of about forty-five, but as a teenager, pale-faced with a wide-mouthed smile. It was the most recent picture they had because he went missing nearly thirty years ago, shortly after Clifford Olson went to prison. We'd moved away, and it wasn't until they began digging up dirt to lay down new foundations at the school that Vincent's bones were found.

I wanted to see where he was buried. When I arrived in town, I almost missed the turnoff because of the construction at the school—it was unrecognizable, like an old tattoo, tattooed over. But the place he was buried was easy to find. There was no police flagging tape or cones, but at the back of the field was a cluttered monument. Photos paper-clipped to twine hung from the limb of a fir tree nearby, store-bought bouquets, still in the cellophane, lay in a pile, and rocks held letters down, some of them older and soggy now from rain. "I miss your laugh," one said. "We miss you, Turtle King!" said another. I decided to drive to our old house, the one with shingle siding, always dusted with crane flies, damp and drooping by the river. I wouldn't have remembered the name of the road if Mom hadn't mentioned it the last time we talked. We talked a couple of times a year. She would tell me about a good taco stand or some article on DNA in *Scientific American*, and I would bore her with complaints about my landlord, the way she lectured the tenants with so many exclamation points in her notes about pot smell in the hallways. But in this call, Mom told me I should buy the old "Stelly Road house."

"You remember—next to Gwen in the houseboat," she said.

"But I work in the city."

I could hear her smoking, exhaling into the phone. Then she said she had to go because someone was at the door, which sounded weird to me, the word "door," because she lived in an Airstream trailer in Mexico. But I guess it was a door.

It was less than three kilometres to my old house, down only two roads bordered by hydro poles. I wasn't expecting the first road to be paved. On the right, a large sign with a red arrow pointed to the U-Pick pumpkin farm ahead. There were a few cars parked there, tables of fresh produce and honey outside, and a couple with a small child holding hands like paper dolls, wandering through the pumpkins. In the browning vines, the orange globes looked like a field of beheaded revolutionaries. I couldn't remember the house that used to be there, and I didn't think that was such a strange thing—I was only six years old when we moved away. I remembered something about a man who beat his wife, although I never saw them. Still, there were lots of neighbours I didn't know.

"He'll get his," Mom said once about the man, passing her cigarette to Gwen.

Gwen looked like a witch to me as a child, with her long grey-ing hair on her young face, as if she was halfway to transitioning out of a disguise. She was really skinny, too, which made me think she was not the maternal type, but Mom was soft all over, with a large chest like down. It might have been the way Gwen always crossed one leg over the other, tucking her foot behind her ankle, all wrapped together as if nothing could touch her. I saw my mom kiss her on the cheek once, which made Gwen even more of a mystery. Her husband, Mike, on the other hand, was a friendly Sasquatch with his giant auburn beard, forever in swim trunks, Mister Fun. "God gonna smite him for us?" Gwen said, and blew smoke rings up to the ceiling.

When I turned left at the U-Pick, the only possible direction down Stelly Road, gravel crunched under the tires just like it always had. The cedar hedges Mom planted had grown up, so I couldn't see our old house or the field behind. I wondered if it was still full of nothing but stumps, yarrow, dandelions, tall grasses, blackberries way at the back, marking the end of our property like barbed wire. I used to call that place the Stump Woods. It might have been a sad scene, a single child playing in this mutilated forest, but there was an old hydro tower that lay on its side back there, too, which became giant playground bars, or a spaceship, a jail, a labyrinth with a Mi-notaur. I didn't usually have an audience, but Mom was out there more often just before we moved away. "Just making sure you're still here," she said.

"I'm going to feed you to the Minotaur!" I stalked toward her, cramping my fingers up so they looked like claws. It was hard to get a rise out of Mom. She was like a train, a steady speed and a puff of smoke to let you know she's coming, always on her way to the next destination. I tugged her arm, but she twisted out of my hold, her mind already elsewhere. She put one foot on a stump. "Someone had plans for this land," she said.

She was finally right, because there was a sign out front

indicating the property had been rezoned for subdividing and was for sale.

It was nearly ten years ago when Mom phoned me to say the place was gone.

"You sold it?" I said.

"I lost it. I gotta pay five thousand a month for Mom's nursing home—who has five thousand a month, for chrissakes." I guess she lost her mother that year, too.

"I didn't even know you still had it," I said. A month later, she'd moved to Mexico.

The mint-coloured house across the road looked the same, except without any of the potted geraniums that used to border the driveway. This was where the old lady and her son lived. She used to tease her hair up like coconut cotton candy, pink scalp visible beneath, which matched the pink sweat suits she always wore. Even though she was really old, it seemed as though she looked after her son, and not the other way around. She'd be dead now. Her son must be lonely—unless I got that wrong. Maybe he was a loser who bounced from one job to another, getting fired for things like showing up late, or mouthing off the boss because he thought he was someone who always knew better, so he had no choice but to freeload off his sweet mother. Maybe he was even happy when she passed away, because then he had the house to himself, celebrated with a night out at the Fraser Arms Pub.

All Mom ever drank was Coke. Gwen, too. Mike had more eclectic tastes, imported things in oddly shaped bottles. I remembered sitting at the picnic table on the dock next to their houseboat, playing Sorry! with Gwen and Mike, and eating Triscuits with mango chutney. Some might have described Mike as a prankster.

"Mallory," he said, emerging from the houseboat. "Got a special treat for ya." He handed me a cracker with green sauce. I was a big fan of salsa verde. "Made your favourite," he said.

But he'd put habanero sauce on it. I panted like a dog, my eyes watering. Mike laughed with that big belly sound. It might have seemed like a mean joke to play on a six-year-old, except he handed me his beer, said, "Atta girl!"

Gwen snatched the bottle from me. "Stop it," she said, almost hissing. I wasn't sure if she was talking to me or Mike.

Sometimes small towns know who done it before the police. Like Pickton, the guy from Port Coquitlam who murdered all those women. According to Mom, when she was a kid—decades before the news caught up to him—there were rumours that he'd drowned a kid in a ditch. Mom talked about him like he was bad weather, surprising, but also expected. "Don't think police are always there to help," she told me.

If Gwen and Mike were still living in the houseboat, I thought they might have some theories about Vincent. I thought I'd want to know. For a while, before we moved, I couldn't get out of my bed if the lights in my room weren't on. I'd call Mom to come turn them on so I could go to the bathroom. I was afraid that if I stepped down, a sharp hand would reach out and grab me, spear me, and hook its nails around my ankle bone. It was Mom who made me look under the bed.

Once, Mom and Gwen and Mike were talking about a "proper burial" for the children Clifford Olson murdered. I can guess, now, how this came up, with the controversy about Olson's family getting ten thousand dollars for each body he guided the police to.

"The families need to bury them," Gwen said, twisting her long hair into a knot.

Mike picked at his toenail, shaking his head. "What do you know about it?"

"She knows they need a grave," Mom said.

"And ol' Cliff gets a trust fund for his kiddie."

Mom told me not to talk to strangers, which wasn't difficult—I never saw any. "There are bad people everywhere," she said.

I'd only learned about Stranger Danger, cautionary tales told in the form of upbeat songs sung by children, which I made up dances to. "Everywhere?" I said, turning my hands into binoculars and scanning the dock. Mom told me to run up to the house and get her another Coke from the fridge.

I couldn't remember any of the names of any of my neighbours after we moved away from the farm house. We lived in an apartment building in town, and then a house in the suburbs, but all those kids looked dangerous to me. "Is that your mom or your dad?" one kid asked me. "Mom," I said. I don't think there was a right answer.

On my bike rides, I'd sometimes see Vincent at the end of Stelly Road, sitting on a round of a log, reading a paperback and eating Whoppers. He had fidgety hands and big pimples on his chin and forehead, which always stood out so much because his skin was so pale, almost blue it was so pale, but his voice was hoarse so that when he talked, he sounded like a dog with something stuck in its throat.

"Are you a stranger?" I asked him once.

"You know my name," he smiled, and returned to his paperback. On the cover was a creature with a human body and a lizard head in the middle of battle, a scene made obvious by its pained expression, lizard tongue hanging out like ribbon, empty human hand, splayed, slightly webbed, and a laser falling away. "He's shot," Vincent explained. "Don't worry—he gets taken to the hospital and fixed up."

"Where do you live?" I asked.

Vincent popped a Whopper in his mouth, looked past me at the field of corn, then leaned forward. "Earth. For now," he whispered. This wasn't funny to me at the time. It was mysterious.

Now that I'm an adult, I don't know my neighbours, either. There was a loud thumping upstairs once, and I wondered if someone was being beaten and if I should call the police, but there was no shouting. I thought Mom and Gwen must've seen bruises on the man's wife—we were all too far away to hear anything. But how much noise would a hammer to the head make?

From far away, the houseboat looked the same as it did when I was six: blue, green deck, a mobile of shells. I expected Gwen to come out in a thinning cotton T-shirt and jean shorts, even though it was late October, the dock the colour of slate.

Closer, the wooden siding showed its age, warped in places. The Astroturf on the deck only looked like soggy carpet, or a dirty Band-Aid to cover a festering porch.

"Hello!" I called. There were steps inside the boat, and then Gwen opened the door. Her cheeks were fuller, and she'd put on weight around the middle.

"Hello," she smiled, not in a friendly way, but like a tired sales clerk. Then, "Mallory, my God, look at you."

"You look the same." I was surprised she recognized me. "I was passing through, thought I'd say hi."

Gwen nodded, fingered an oyster shell and the mobile clapped gently. "Well hello to you, too, stranger."

"How are you?" I said.

"Good." I waited for her to expand on this, or ask me about Mom, how she was doing. But Gwen just nodded in the way people do when they listen to music, as if agreeing with it.

"Where's Mike?" I asked.

Her eyes widened. "I don't know," she said, and wrapped her arms around herself, one hand on her shoulder as if she were cold. "I been married and divorced since, that's how long you been away."

"Yeah, it's been a while." I fiddled with some tissue in my pocket.

"But I'm surprised you made it down the dock without crying this time!" she laughed. "You were so afraid of Mike after he pushed your mother in the water."

"You mean because of the dog?"

Mike threw our dog in the water to "teach her how to swim," and the dog did swim, but she had big white crescent moons around her eyes. When she reached the dock, she couldn't jump up so she just paddled frantically at the side until finally Mike grabbed her scruff with one hand and put the other under her rear end to lift her up, but the dog squeaked as he pulled her onto the dock. As she was about to shake the water off, Mike shoved her with his thonged foot.

"You're not getting me wet!" he laughed. Mom threw an orange at him and Mike bolted at her, pushed her in before she had the chance to move. It seemed like a funny story, crazy summer days at the dock or something.

"I wouldn't say I was afraid of him," I said.

"No? I guess you were pretty little back then." She looked away as she said this, as if the comment was for someone else. It reminded me how she would glance silently at Mom when I asked her questions like how to do a braid, or why her hair was grey, and Mom would tell me to go play upstairs.

Gwen looked down the dock, then across the river at the white church on the reservation. "It's nice to see you, Mallory, but I'm expecting a phone call, so I should probably head inside."

I told her it was nice to see her, too, and that was it. I had an ill feeling, as if I'd just embarrassed myself, but I'd done nothing wrong. I never even asked about Vincent. If I had, perhaps Mom wouldn't have misunderstood me.

I looked up the river. Logs lost from booms cluttered both sides, the odd brown bottle sticking out of the mud, but it smelled good. Maybe anything familiar smells good: sweet and grassy, blend of citrus and spicy earthiness: corn. Curry and tobacco: Mom. I wondered what she smelled like now. Ocean? Lime and beer sweat? Did she feed pelicans on the beach, or put out leftovers for the stray dogs? She used to feed the crows potato chips, which was funny when I thought of how many scarecrows were crucified in the corn fields around us. She came to my school once and confronted some kid who made fun of my glasses, poked him in the chest with each syllable and the kid never bothered me again. I liked watching her smoke, the way it swirled up past her nose and thick owl eyebrows.

"You have an owl head," I said. Then she called me her little owlet, but reminded me I still had to be inside before dark.

She never had any advice for me in those phone calls from Mexico. She never told me anything really—nothing of substance. I had the arrogance to think it was something to do with me, as if she was just waiting for me to reach out to her first.

A loud smack hit the water and I turned to see the dark head of a beaver swimming away. I thought of Vincent, and imagined this beaver with a human body, and any moment it would dive down by lifting its fleshy buttocks up and kicking with two long legs. It was as though the beaver heard me thinking, because it dove under, revealing its fat, dark furred body as it went.

Gwen did seem odd to me that day. I hadn't seen her in nearly thirty years, yet our conversation was so casual, as if she'd expected me to drop by sooner or later. But I was never good at understanding what's in people's heads. Maybe not even as a child. After all, the boy in those photos at the monument was not how I'd remembered him. In one, Vincent wore what looked like a gold lamé curtain, turned up at the collar like a cloak, carried by two kids with their hands clasped underneath. In another, he was on all fours, a child of about four or five riding him like a pony. Another, Vincent at about ten in a family photo by a pool, everyone raising cups in a toast, but Vincent with his eyes crossed and tongue out, fingers up like antennae.

All I remembered was a strange kid, sitting on that log with a paperback. I guess he wouldn't have been very strong. Long fingers would reach up, try to push into eye sockets, but slipping on some wet face, until knees pin his arms, grown-up hands wrapped around Vincent's slim neck.

I was afraid of Clifford Olson the first time I heard his name, but this was also after he'd been arrested, so there was nothing to fear. What if Vincent was the twelfth to die, a secret not even money could buy, I thought. But this was impossible.

I headed down the stairs from the dike, over the footbridge, with horsetail growing up beneath it, all prehistoric. Those were whips for jailers at the hydro tower.

A crow sat on top of the rezoning sign, nodding its head up down, up down, its wings almost mantling. I stopped at the sign. "I have no chips for you, crow." It made the sound of a drum roll, but guttural. A flock of red-winged blackbirds lifted off the corn nearby, turning south, then north, then shifting westward toward the Stump Woods, perpetually undecided.

The Stump Woods is the place I remembered most, I guess, the yellow grass curtaining stumps, swaying, a soft yet unyield-ing noise. I used to pretend I was a cat hunting mice, or I'd be the mouse, imagining a feline stalker. Crouch in the grass, the mouse tip-toes past, looks up, sniffs the air, listens, the crunch of sneakers on the dike, wind, nothing else, then the cat leaps from its hiding spot, devours the mouse—unless it makes it to the Safety Stump. Either way, the mouse becomes the cat, and even the stump could be hiding something.

"No cats here," I said aloud. It's amazing how a rezoning sign can transform a wild place into an empty lot. Mom was right: someone had plans for this land. The stumps would come up, the blackberries torn out. The hydro tower moved, maybe. I buried a corn husk doll there once. A mouse Mom caught in a trap got a ceremony, too. A candy stash—a shoebox full of Halloween toffees that went soggy in the damp soil. What else was here? There could be markers—a ribbon on the hydro tower, a stick in the ground, a cairn, a crop circle. Stranger things had happened. I held my hands up to my eyes like binoculars: serial killers and missing kids, weird neighbours, some wife-beater. And what was their story? Did he move his wife to some tiny house, surrounded by corn shuffling in the breeze so no one can hear her crying out for help? Did he buy her bunches of daffodils from the IGA after? Did he go too far one night, tell his friends she took off, pretend to be angry about this?

I used to get so worn out by tragedies—a jogger in the park, a stolen child, someone randomly attacking women at bus stops. Then there are links to articles, police warnings on how to stay safe. All those headlines disappear after a week, and I never know if they even catch the man, or whoever it is. Still, I keep my keys in my hand when I walk to my car, but not to open a door faster. I make a fist around them, with one point out.

I turned toward the corn field, and then the scarecrows looked like spies, or gothic grave markers saying, "Over here!" Was this how Mom felt, I wondered, suddenly surrounded by horror? Maybe this was why we moved to the plastic house in the suburbs. And when this place was finally gone, she left town for good.

"Adiós," she said, and joked that she had all the Spanish she needed. "Dos cervezas, por favor!" There was something phony in her laugh, because she never drank beer, or at least, not while I lived with her.

There was a car in the driveway of the mint house which I hadn't noticed before. I wondered if it could be the same man that had lived there with his mother. I wanted to ask him about Vincent, or the other man, or if Mike was still in town. The missing and murdered were adding up. Who knows what's out there, I thought. In the suburbs, I walked quickly to school, keeping as far from the road as I could, worried about a car pulling over and an arm yanking me inside. A babysitter told me once that Clifford Olson had killed a child with a pitch fork, and after that, I imagined him in coveralls, hay in his hair, like a farmer, like any farm neighbour, or a scarecrow, but in a car on every highway, in every cul-de-sac. Mike said Clifford Olson was only famous because nothing interesting went on here.

"Don't get all worked up about it," he said, knuckling Gwen in the ribs. "There's worse things than a few dead kids."

"D'you mind?" Mom said. She blew smoke in his direction, then butted her cigarette right there on the picnic table.

Mike scratched his beard as he looked at Mom, then Gwen, back to Mom. "Huh," he said.

I handed Mom her Coke. "Here you are, sir," I joked.

I was about to walk over to the mint house and knock when the door opened. It was Gwen, and she was speaking to someone just inside, but it was too dark to see who she was speaking to. She stayed at the door talking to a shadowy figure, not completely obscured—the person was tall, with white hands, but that was all I saw. I didn't want her to think I was spying, although I was beginning to wonder if she really had been expecting a call. I walked alongside the corn, toward the U-Pick and the place Vincent used to sit.

I used to know how to make a doll out of corn husks, and now I never even buy corn on the cob. I used to eat it raw when I was a kid, just rip it off the stem. It was slightly chalky, but still sweet. Maybe I just got sick of it. Gwen showed me how to pull the smoother, more flexible inner leaves from the husks, the sticky feel of it, the chunky tear when I pull them from the base. She twisted pieces into rope-like legs and fanned out other pieces for wings, flying people, yellowing and then browning in the sun. She gave me one. This was meant to be nice, maybe, but to me, it was witchcraft.

When I showed Vincent this doll, he told me about voodoo, to entertain me, maybe, because now I know he was funny, but at the time, I thought he was a serious boy. I didn't want to have this voodoo doll because it was a fairy, and if fairies were things I should want to harm with this magic, then perhaps this meant they were dangerous. After all, why would you harm something that wasn't threatening you? So I buried it in the Stump Woods, by the hydro tower.

"Why did you do that, Mallory? Now it can't breathe," Vincent said. But he probably didn't say that. That didn't sound like the kid people remembered, I thought, so maybe I made that part up, imagined it. Gwen was right—it had been a long time. Maybe I knew Vincent was goofy, but just couldn't remember, like I couldn't remember being afraid of Mike when I was a kid.

At the end of the road, where Vincent used to sit, the log was gone. Nothing was there but a stop sign. I walked toward the

U-Pick barn, which looked new when I had driven past it earlier. Up close, there were grey streaks of lichen and moss on the exterior. There was no house there, just a portable home, an office for the U-Pick and a place to store tables. I remembered Vincent on the log with his paperback, pointing to the barn. "Hide in there," he said. He could have said that.

I went in, even though it was dark inside. It looked like an old stable for horses, no cement, just ground. Then I remembered there used to be a couch here, a brown couch. When I turned around, the white sky blinded me for a second, until my eyes adjusted, but then the walls of the barn were indiscernible, simply black, so it was just a black frame around Stelly Road. I could just barely see the top of my house above the corn. I remembered hiding here once when Gwen was at my house. She was red-faced, eyes swollen like bee stings. Her hands cupped over her own mouth like she was trying to quiet herself. Mom held her hand, moved the grey hair from her damp face, shushed her.

"Bring me a cloth," Mom said, or "Bring me some ice."

Mom smoothing her thumb back and forth on the top of Gwen's hand. Gwen crying but her mouth in an ugly smile. "Get upstairs!" Rumbling voices. Shouting. Something slamming. Quiet. I sneaked downstairs, peeked around the corner. Gwen and Mom were standing, Mom whispering, eyes like a wax figure. The way they stood there, they looked unmoored, floating, exchanging whispers like spells. Was this a memory, or some story, all mixed up? I wasn't sure if Gwen really noticed me hiding behind that corner, if she didn't say anything, just leaned her head on Mom's shoulder, and if I went out the back door to my bike, pedalled to Vincent.

When I came out of the barn, a man was putting three pumpkins in his trunk. I pictured Clifford Olson in an orange jumpsuit like a jack-o-lantern, breath streaming from nostrils and crystallizing in the cold, but hand-cuffed, guiding the police through towering forests and sword ferns, boots on needles, remembering. The man drove away, and then there were no more cars parked outside, and the family like paper dolls had gone, too. I headed back to the mint house. The door was closed, so I knocked, quick and loud. Heavy steps came toward it, then it opened.

Her hair was longer and lighter, not with grey, but just a diminishing vibrance. What was once deep brown was now more like corn silk. Her face sagged under her chin, but other than that, she looked the same.

"So you found me," my mother said.

I couldn't say anything. I don't know if I was angry, or just shocked to find her there. I tried to piece together something to say, but I'd forgotten for that moment what it was I'd expected to find in the first place.

"I haven't been here long," she said. "Just a rental."

The son—the son with the dead mother, Vincent, Mike. I shook my head. I still had no words.

She slid her hands into her pockets, nodding. "I guess you want to come in?" There was a pumpkin on the table behind her, its top cut out and sitting next to it.

"Are you carving a pumpkin?" I said finally, as if this made everything worse. And it did make it worse, because once I'd said that, I couldn't stop talking. What happened to the old lady? How could you come here and not tell me? How could Gwen lie to my face?

"And I know about Mike. And I know about you and Gwen, too."

She leaned back, each syllable pushing her, jab, jab, jab. "What?"

"How could you have been friends with him?"

She looked past me, as if she was expecting a visitor. "I cared about Gwen."

"Yes, I know that," I said.

She looked at her feet, the way I do when I don't know what to say. "What do you want from me?"

"Nothing."

She stared at me, and I stared back. It was stupid, like two cats meeting each other on the dike, waiting for the other to look away. "Then why are you here, Mallory?" she said, her chin jutting forward as if the answer would reach her faster this way.

My stomach turned, and I glanced at the pile of pumpkin innards on the table, which looked like an omen now, or a warning, or a clue. I imagined the pumpkin turning around to look at me, but it had no face yet. It couldn't speak or open its eyes so it only undulated, trying desperately to tear itself a mouth. I thought of Vincent. "I just wanted to see where he was buried."

The blackbirds chirped over the house toward the river. She watched them go, then looked past me at our old driveway. She shook her head, as if she could cast off the question. "It was a different time," she said, as though it required no other justification.

"That's it?" I said. I think I'd had enough of casual conversations, polite evasions. Life is a disaster—child killers get pensions. I told her she was self-centred. I'm sure I called her a bitch, worse. I wanted her to be sorry, tell me how awful it is, how fucked up. I said, "He was someone we knew. I spent time with him. And he's been buried here this whole time, no one knowing, and you're just back from Mexico with your fucking tan and that's it? Let's go carve a pumpkin?"

"Mike was a fucking bully, so cool it. Didn't even know what hit him. I'd tell you it was an accident but I thought about putting him in that ground way too many times for that to make any fucking sense."

I laughed. Stopped laughing. "I was talking about Vincent."

I was a child on the verge of a tantrum, a heat rolling up from my gut like hot hands on my neck, then my mouth, nose, making it hard to breathe. I wanted to tear grass out, throw rocks, kick, run, fight, fly. I turned away, took a breath.

"Jesus Christ, Mallory."

In some ways, nothing changed—nothing had changed. The crow nodded again from the top of the rezoning sign.

"They're gonna dig over there," Mom said, walking back toward the pumpkin on the table, muttering about the stumps coming out after all these years.

I wonder if it was nighttime when Vincent died. If he looked around the schoolyard, heard the rustling in the corn behind, said, "I know this place." I guess I'll never know. I think of Clifford Olson. Clifford Olson, Clifford Olson. Don't look in the mirror. But he simply died of cancer in a quiet hospital room.

I followed her inside.

The Sign

Ruth is the last one. She takes the linen serviette by two corners and snaps it, firing dust particles into the room, which she can't see because it's too dark, the sun is setting, but she can feel them tingle her mucous membrane. In the room: three bunks, six beds, five friends. She drapes the last serviette over William's face. Now it is her turn to drink.

They sat at the kitchen table the night before crushing up the pills with stone mortars and tapping the dust into a bowl. Today they added the apple juice, sparkling water and vodka. It was Ruth's job to ensure the successful launch, or to administer more if needed. Shallow breathing still. Then one of them called out to her, "Ruth!" It was Don.

His eyes swirled in their sockets, but he was too weak to sit up. Ruth placed her hand on his heart. His sweatshirt was damp. "But we have to leave," she said. "I am right behind you. Can't you see the ship?"

"I can't see anything, Ruth! I can't see anything!"

"Not yet—soon."

In a bunk nearby, William was silent, hands at his sides, palms up. His wife was already there, he'd announced months ago, waiting for them on the next planet.

Don's chest is finally still. They must be there now, Ruth thinks. She pictures Captain Kirk, pea-yellow tunic and boomerang patch, his walkie-talkie. Beam me up, Scotty. Ruth always played Spock as a kid. She liked to say to her brother, "Ah yes, one of your Earth emotions."

It won't be like that, though. Ruth looks up to the window, which is high on the wall so only the sky can be seen. There is still too much sun, but Hale-Bopp is up there, guiding the ship to the next planet. She closes her eyes to listen. A plane or a helicopter somewhere, but in here, quiet. Everything she needs is waiting for her.

She leaves the bedroom door open and returns to the kitchen.

William's eyebrows rose like two puffy clouds when he heard about the UFO three months ago. The radio DJ has since undermined this claim by interviewing that Hawaiian physics professor, but this is not the first time people have failed to read the signs, William said. Ruth knows this is true. Like the time she went hiking in the dry hills behind the campground, past the yellow sign, "Caution: Snakes in Area." It was lucky the snake bit her before she'd wandered too far.

She ladles the punch into a plastic cup. A few drops spill on her fingers, which look swollen and red around the knuckles. When did she get her mother's hands? The spilled punch will make her hands sticky, and this will aggravate her, like the sticky keyboard at work. It's that guy with the strawberry hair who's always got a Dixie cup of jujubes or Skittles on him. Why can't he eat on his breaks? Ruth smiles as she turns her hands under the cool tap, then squeezes a drop of dish soap into her palm, lathers, rinses, dries them on the checkered tea towel hanging on the oven handle. Cups with crescent moons of punch at the bottom clutter the counter tops, so Ruth stacks them in a tower beside the sink. Maybe she should throw them in a bag for recycling. That would be the considerate thing to do for the vacation rental company. She'll clean them now. She'll just clean the cups first. It won't take long.

Thomas Bopp sent a Western Union telegram to the Central Bureau for Astronomical Telegrams after spotting the comet through a friend's telescope. Alan Hale had already emailed the bureau three times by the time Bopp's message arrived. But it doesn't matter, understand? It arrived.

Ruth prefers email to the phone. She rinses out the plastic cups and turns them upside down to dry on the tea towel. Waste not. There's only the text to consider, code forming patterns of light forming letters forming words forming sentences. Done. There. Cups are clean. Want not.

But the wrist of one sleeve is wet now. The grey sweat suit is brand new, the inside still soft and fleecy. She ordered them three weeks ago for this purpose, so it is spotless except for this wet sleeve which reminds Ruth of children who suck on the necks of their T-shirts. Is that any way to go? Neutral colours, William said. We are on the threshold of the end of this civilization—it is about to be recycled. Bring nothing but your minds.

Okay. Okay. She takes her cup again. It won't be easy being the last one, William said. You won't see us leave, you will just see us die.

"I don't have to see it to know it's true." Like the loose rock on the old trail. We must go where no man has gone before, her brother said. But Jim! The signs are there for a reason! "He almost died that day," she told William.

"Everything is ephemeral here," he smiled, and touched her shoulder gently, like a grandfather.

Ruth looks into her cup. The bubbles of carbon rise to the top and pop on the apple-yellow surface like sun spots. Pop, pop, pop. She thinks of bubble gum, Bazooka Joe, rocket ship to the moon where everything is black and white, where space travel looks like TVs in living rooms. The Challenger explosion as if we'll never leave Earth again. But now we don't have to, they say. The Hubble has led to impossible discoveries—the rate of expansion of the universe, confirmation of black holes, extrasolar planets. And we can see all of this, everything from home. The world on a keyboard, linked by an invisible web, fibre optics sparkling underground and overhead like technological connective tissue, the human genome almost mapped, even the power to create life co-opted by scientists in lab coats, but what do they create, on the threshold of a new civilization, with the power of life in a petri dish, from a single mammary gland cell, what do they create?

Pop, pop, pop. "A sheep," Ruth says. "They make sheep."

It is time to go, it is. The time is now. So Ruth will just step outside, look outside one last time, locate Hale-Bopp in the northern sky, take a picture for her mind. It's in Andromeda now, and the sun is low enough to see her, chained to a rock light years away. Perseus never gets any closer, not in this lifetime.

From the front steps, Ruth has a view of the entire valley. Ocean view, quiet neighbourhood, perfect for a family getaway. Good choice, Ruth, we will have a peaceful launch. Palm trees rise between red-tiled roofs, forming a suburban canopy in the hazy coastal warmth. The sun has drained away, and the taller palms are silhouetted against the luminous haze of the city, swaying lazily in the breeze as the temperature drops. It is quiet except for the sound of a basketball dribbling in a driveway somewhere. I have heard this sound so many times, Ruth thinks. But the rhythmic smacking on asphalt does not sound like a drum roll. It doesn't sound at all like anything important is about to happen.

Seventeen days ago there was a total solar eclipse in China, Mongolia and Siberia. The moon moved in front of the sun like a thumb, and the only light was a subdued glow along the horizon, a ring around the lawn chairs and tour buses and photographers and curious souls who gathered in the desert. And Hale-Bopp was visible. The last comet seen with a solar eclipse was spotted in July thirty-four years ago. She looked it up. Then the sun returned, and the people went home.

This is not the first time people have failed to read the signs.

She squints at the asphalt roads and cul-de-sacs below for signs of movement, for the basketball, maybe, one last thing to see. Pairs of headlights begin to appear, moving slowly past parked cars, turning into driveways. It is the end of a work day. There are two children sitting on the hood of an old car, lit up by the tungsten glow through a bay window. Are they playing cards? A kid she used to play with would cheat: These are wild now, so I win. Ruth took the card and stuffed it between the sofa cushions. Don't be such a baby, Ruth. That was so long ago—it was a king. He said the kings were wild now. But where was she that day in July?

Think.

The eclipse. Thirty-four years ago ...

Hale-Bopp is brightening in the sky, the blue ion tail pointing away from the sun. This way, it says. This way. But where was she that day in July?

This way, Ruth, she hears William say.

"I can have one more minute, can't I?" And the comet must wrap around the sun before it makes its way back, at tens of thousands of miles per hour. Can the others feel that velocity now? She pictures them bracing themselves against a riveted wall, cupping their ears against the noise like tots at air shows when jets exceed the speed of sound and the noise rips the sky apart. Or maybe the room is white and padded for their protection because there is less gravity, and their elbows are hooked so they stay together and they spin in circles, but there is still so much noise, so much noise, so they are vibrating like hammered bells with pairs of eyes here, and here, and here, and here, and here. Or maybe they are dead quiet. Still. Floating like dish soap bubbles through a summer day.

This way, Ruth.

Like that day in July, before Jim and Spock, before we got the TV, when we had to go outside to see the stars. She remembers chomping through poster paper with red-handled scissors, white glue and aluminum foil, the teacher with her Styrofoam ball, the moon, moving in front of the foam one, the sun, explaining about the moon's shadow, the umbra, elliptical orbits, but Ruth can't remember the eclipse at all. She can't remember it at all.

Maybe the ship is just as Ruth always imagined one. They are peering out portholes, looking for the houses they used to live in which look like tiny dollhouses from so high, and look how small the cars are. I think I see my school. Wait—where is Ruth?

This way, Ruth, this way.

But she is microscopic. She is a single cell. She is someone on the dark side of the planet now, wondering how she could have missed the sun go out.

The Things I Would Say

I was six weeks pregnant, sitting in my reclining chair, staring at the tweed upholstered couch on the other side of the room, trying to imagine an infant on it. Maybe wrapped in the brown and orange crocheted shawl draped over the back of the couch. There was a cigarette burn on the couch's arm. I needed to quit smoking, but I was trying on this idea of motherhood first. I had to say the words, feel them in my mouth, hear them before I knew if it was possible. Me, a mother. I am a mother. That's my baby wrapped up in the cro-chet shawl over there. But if it were on the couch, maybe I should sit beside it, so it wouldn't fall and smash its skull on the hardwood floor. Knock on wood.

Even in my daydreams I said the wrong thing. And then, of course, I thought of my sister, Lily, not as she looked the last time I saw her, but as a kid, her white-blonde hair and fat cheeks, little blue eyes like marbles. She was coming over and she'd be here soon, but not to drive me to my appointment. That was at two. I had less than an hour to change my mind if I wanted. This was just one of Lily's usual stops on her way to or from visiting Dad.

"You can come, you know," she'd say.

I would say "No, it's okay." Sometimes she asked why. "Not everyone wants to visit their parents, Lily. It's not that unusual."

I looked at the empty couch and crossed my arm over my abdo-men, as if I needed to shield this fetus or embryo, I wasn't sure what it was called just yet. I imagined Lily's mouth opening wider, then wider, as if it was about to swallow the room.

"Dad's doing a lot better," she'd said on the phone.

"Better than what?"

"He can move around again."

I'd forgotten he was in a motorcycle accident, hit at a four-way stop and left with a broken collarbone. I was more surprised by the fact he owned a motorcycle than that he'd been the victim of a hit and run. It was hard to picture that old man, with his greasy, thinning hair and plaid fleece jackets, riding along country roads all summer, stopping off at fruit stands, stuffing his face with peaches as though he could be so carefree.

When I was a kid, a teacher told me that family was forever— that blood was thicker than water. She thought this was a comfort.

We were together all the time back then, partly the result of divorce, partly because we lived in a trailer—no TV, no phone, just bikes and trailer park kids. The river. One of the old ladies in the park would cluck her tongue at us when she saw us playing. "Look at that hair," she'd say, shaking her head. "You have to braid it your-self, don't you?" Sometimes she gave us popsicles for the privilege of saying this.

We baptized each other one summer, my sister Lily, and Krista from the "stick and staple," as my dad called the fibreglass trailers. It wasn't a Christian baptism—we made a coven, obviously, because there were three of us. We dressed up in all black and called ourselves the Sturgeon Coven. Krista wore black spandex and a T-shirt, too hot for summer, and extended her tanned arms, eyes closed to the sun. Lily and I kneeled in the mud in front of her with our palms turned up.

"O! From the depths and millions of years, ancient monsters that no one ever saw! We call on your powers—give them to us!" Krista walked toward the river, the mud squelching beneath her sneakers.

"You first," she said to me. I took off my flip-flops and we waded deeper into the river. The current swelled past, like watery ribbons around my waist.

"O! Sturgeon! Rise up! Rise up and take this woman," she said. Lily and I laughed. Krista was always calling us women, not girls, and it was funny. "Take this woman on your cosmic journey to the depths! She offers her soul!"

Now we laughed maniacally, recognizing the absurdity of a cosmic sturgeon, but also the frightening possibility of the magic of her words, that they might work. I pinched my nose and Krista pushed my shoulders down, holding me there for a moment, unexpectedly, long enough for me to notice the silence under water, nothing to conceal a sound. What would I hear? It could be watching me now, with my eyes clamped shut. What if I opened them? It would sway just below and I'd wonder if it was only my own shadow, then the flash of its diamond-backed skin, but too fast to recognize. Suddenly, its face to my face, jelly eyes bulging at the sides, or black marble shark-eyes, grey lips, teeth, ready to snap my soul and guide me to the darkness. I tried to get my footing on the slippery mud, but I was just past the drop-off. Let me up, let me up! I flailed, splashed toward Krista, found my footing and stood.

I was invigorated, not angry with her at all for this near drowning, not angry at all with how close I came to my soul being taken by the sturgeon. My sister's turn. She was not happy about it, though. She told us we were assholes. It was the first time I'd heard her swear.

"It's just a joke," Krista called as Lily walked up the bank, through the poplars toward the trailers.

Krista was twelve, nearly two years older than me. She knew how to roll a cigarette and what a blow job was, but as she watched Lily go, Krista's brows knitted together as if she were confused, and I realized I understood some things better than her. Like ceremony. Fat scabs pocked her arm where she'd picked at mosquito bites. Didn't she know that only made a bite last longer? Her sneakers were soaked, heavy-looking. Why had she not bothered to take them off?

"What?" she asked.

"Nothing. It's your turn."

I thought the sturgeon had pulled me out past the drop-off. I thought it wanted me to come to the bottom of the river, like a mermaid. But I didn't fantasize about long hair and seashell bras. Why pretend to be anything that glamorous? We knew what we were—we saw it in the other people at the trailer park, like Krista's mom with the hoarse voice and yellow fingers, who was rarely home, who sat out front sometimes rolling cigarettes and getting her feet massaged by her boyfriend with the jean jacket.

Krista put her hands together like a prayer, and closed her eyes. "Ready," she said.

I put my hands on her shoulders, and jumped before pushing down. It took no effort, because she really dunked herself, but once she was under water, I pushed her forhead so she was back to the mud and held her down horizontal, her long, slippery body like a Barbie, but spongy. I thought of our toys: Lego people with plastic helmets for hair, plastic horses with realistic proportions, a brass frog, and one Barbie with purple scribbles on her face. The Lego people didn't fit on the horse, so Barbie usually rode it, too tall so the balls of her toeless feet touched the ground. I'd said she'd lost her toes in a bike accident which is why she needed a horse to carry her around.

Lily had looked worried by this. She took Barbie and smoothed back the knotted polyester hair, as if by saying this, I had actually inflicted the pain of the accident on Barbie.

It wasn't that long that I held Krista there, but when her feet finally got hold in the mud and she jumped up, she shoved me.

"What are you doing?!" she shouted. Then she cried and smacked the water at me, instead of hitting my face.

I got angry back. "It's not a joke! You were being stupid!"

"Fuck you!"

Usually she swore when talking about someone else, like the boy in the motorhome with the Nintendo. He flicked snot at us once when we were riding our bikes. She said he was a fucking asshole and a cocksucker. She explained that a cocksucker was someone who sucked penises and that this was something men liked. I wouldn't have first-hand knowledge of that until I was fifteen, and it would be a couple years more before it didn't feel like a kind of clumsy punishment.

Krista's bad language and sexual knowledge was the only power she'd ever have. I was too young to really be conscious of that fact, but on some level, I knew that was her lot. Not Lily. Maybe because she was polite, it was hard to imagine Lily could be hurt by someone. But I was surprised when she actually finished high school and that was just the beginning. She even had a boyfriend for a few years. I'd ask, "How are things going with what's-his-face?"

Lily would pretend I was joking because what else could she do? "Same. Great." It made no sense to me.

After the baptism incident, Krista played with Lily instead of me, even though they were almost four years apart. Lily would sit outside at the picnic table while I made us grilled cheese sandwiches for our after-school snack. In the time it took for my bread to brown, Krista would come by and lure my sister away.

One of these afternoons, I rode my bike around the park alone and let it fall on the pavement with a metallic clatter when I reached Krista's stick and staple. She was draping an old sheet lengthwise along the brown and white striped awning. My sister was sitting on their picnic table washing Barbie's hair in a bowl of water, the blue jumpsuit unvelcroed beside her. She was gentle even with a plastic doll. Some years later, she would slice up her arm, first like a cat, then more like a surgeon, a kind of healing, though it looked more like an attack, and I would pretend not to notice.

It seemed unlikely that Krista really wanted to play with someone so much younger. Krista saw me standing there with my bike. She said to Lily, "Tell her we're not open yet."

"Tell Barbie?"

"No! The woman outside."

Lily laughed at this and I couldn't stop myself from smiling a little. "We're closed!" my sister chimed.

"I don't want to come in anyway," I said.

Krista was standing on the picnic table bench, reaching up with the corner of the sheet and trying to tuck it between the metal rod and the vinyl awning attached to it, but the bench was not quite high enough to reach this outer edge. She climbed on top of the table to reach, but now she was farther away. She put one hand on the rod and leaned toward it. "We probably won't even be open today," she said. "We have a lot to do to get ready. And even if we are ready, we still might be too busy for new people."

Lily was no longer lathering Barbie's hair. She looked up at me, waiting for me to speak. I was going to come up with something biting, something to put Krista in her place, to let her know that just because she's older doesn't mean she's in charge. She worked at stuffing the corner of the sheet in, with a concentrated, ugly grin on her face. The awning vibrated and I wondered how much weight she could put on the rod without breaking it. Only the tip of the sheet was making it in and she couldn't reach far enough to yank it out from below. She leaned over further, raising one foot up and pointing it out behind her, balancing. Her toenails were red except where the paint was chipping off.

"You're gonna fall," I said. Repeated it.

Krista was puffing away. "No I'm not." She tried to pinch the corner between her fingers.

"Yes you are. You're going to fall, you stupid idiot."

Krista reached again, more forcefully now and yanked at the sheet.

The corner of the sheet must have gotten sweatier every time she grabbed at it. She didn't have a good hold of it. She fell off the table, hitting her shins on the bench and landing on her stomach. She let out a thin howl from getting the wind knocked out of her. Lily left Barbie in the bowl, climbed off the table carefully, and kneeled next to Krista.

"Are you okay?" she said.

Krista couldn't answer because she still couldn't catch a breath. I stood there with my bike, unsure what to do. Dad wasn't home yet and Krista's mom was almost never around. I didn't want to bug anyone else because some of the people in the park were mean and most of them were really old.

"She's fine," I said.

Lily touched Krista's back as Krista managed to squeeze out, "You're dead."

Lily frowned in that clownish way she does just before she starts to cry. "I'm sorry, Krista."

When Krista caught her breath, she sat up on the ground and said, "Not you."

"I'm not dead," I said. Then told my sister, "Come on," and started to walk my bike back to our trailer. She didn't walk beside me, but followed behind. Later, Krista had more to say about it, but not to me.

She lied to my dad. It was true I taunted her, wanted her to fall, wished it, but I never said the other thing, that her mother was a slut. I hadn't even heard the word before my dad said it. In high school, two girls approached me in the hall. "You're a slut," one said, smiling, matter-of-factly. By then, I was used to being branded. I just didn't want to be at home with Dad and Lily, and it was easy enough to hang out at some guy's house.

"A slut?" Dad asked. "Where did you get such a foul mouth?"

I knew it was bad, because he was angry. I wondered if he still loved me, if we would have special time with juice and snacks, like he had with Krista that day. Then he said I was "better than that," that I needed to apologize, that he loved me. In that moment, before everything else happened, I would have done anything for his approval.

Krista didn't come by for a few days after that. She rode up on her bike as Lily and I sat at the picnic table eating grilled cheeses. "It's hot out," she said. "We should go swimming." She was here to pretend nothing had happened.

Lily looked at me, worried. The last time we'd gone in the river was the baptism. "You can make Barbie swim," I offered.

"The fish are sleeping right now," Krista added. "They don't like it when it's hot because it makes them get confused and they bump into log booms. So they stay deep down."

"They don't bump into log booms," I corrected.

"Yes they do."

"Maybe we'll swim by ourselves, at our own beach," I said.

Lily was holding her grilled cheese in both hands. "Krista," she said, "you can have my grilled cheese if you're hungry."

"Don't give it to her!" I whipped her hand, knocking the grilled cheese out so it fell on the dirt.

"Don't tell me what to do!" Lily shouted. She picked up the grilled cheese and dusted it with her hand. The dirt stuck to the greasy bread. She brushed away the needles and chips of bark, but the sandy dirt was embedded in the pores of the bread. If she bit into it, it would be loud and grainy between her teeth. Lily stared at it a moment before she gave up trying to salvage it. "You ruined it," she said.

"Don't cry," I said.

She slapped the grilled cheese back down on the plate in front of her. "You ruined it!"

"Way to go, mommy," Krista said.

"Shut up!" Lily picked up the grilled cheese again and threw it at Krista. It flew past her and landed on the paved road. Lily's face turned red below her white-blonde hair. She thumped up the metal stairs into the trailer and slammed the door. Before Krista and I could say anything to each other, Lily came out again with Barbie and the realistic horse. "I'm going to play by myself!" She turned to walk toward the river and disappeared down the slope into the poplars.

"Well, that was weird," Krista finally announced. She twisted her hands around the handlebars as if she were revving a motorcycle. Then she picked at a leprechaun sticker that had been on the frame so long its ridges had merged with the paint. "You want to go, then?"

It was simpler for Krista to make up and get on with things. She didn't hold grudges. I agreed to go with her, but I thought of myself as a spy, keeping tabs on my enemy. I would report to Lily later all of the terrible stupid things Krista had said so that Lily would remember where her loyalties should lie. So I went with Krista to the beach.

The tide was low, out past the pilings and there was a long yellow-legged bird at the river edge. I followed Krista across the mud toward the log boom. One corner of the boom was practically out of the water completely. I didn't see Lily anywhere. I didn't think about where she had gone at the time, either. I was watching the backs of Krista's legs, long and splattered with mud now, ankle socks in sneakers. She pointed out a blue heron as it flew by, silent except for the heavy downward push of air, which seemed weird to me, that Krista had anything to say about birds. We stopped at a piling to examine the oily surface. Krista squatted to poke holes in the mud with a splinter. The wind had picked up and it felt much cooler than it had in the park, surrounded by metal, fibreglass and asphalt. Swimming had lost its appeal. From upriver, a tug approached, towing a barge like a brick along the brown water. Closer to shore, the heron had landed, its legs half-immersed. The long grey feathers on its chest blew in the wind so that they looked like fingers reaching out.

"They look like dinosaurs when they fly," I said.

"They are dinosaurs. They're related to pterodactyls."

This was another fact she'd invented, like sturgeon facts, and fish swimming into log booms. "You should walk out on the log boom," I said. "It's right up to the beach."

"You walk out."

I didn't say anything right away, then sheepishly, "I'm not

allowed," and feigned embarrassment.

Krista laughed. "Your dad's not even here."

"I'm supposed to set an example." But the beach was empty.

"Let me set an example."

Krista stripped down to her bathing suit, tossing her clothes off like a superhero unveiling her true identity. The suit was thinning around her lower back, the fine white hairs of worn out elastic showing. I didn't see why it was so necessary to take her clothes off. She'd just wanted to make a theatrical approach to the boom, or maybe to see me catch her clothes as she threw them in my direction.

"Watch and learn," she said and stepped onto the boom.

Her long arms extended outward and she stepped carefully from one log to the next. She looked tall and balanced, like the heron, and the wind made her fine hair lash upward along her face. I stood in the mud holding her clothes. The pilings punctuated the distance along the muddy beach. The tug was now passing down the middle of the river.

Krista waved. "Ahoy, Captain!" Then she held both hands up to give him the finger. "Take that, tugboat!"

She walked further out onto the boom until she was right in the middle. I had seen a man walk out there before, as far as the outer edge, to fish, but my dad told Lily and me it wasn't safe.

"Come on, you pussy!"

I looked up the beach. The heron was still standing there, four pilings away. I looked the other way and couldn't see Lily anywhere.

I was really angry at the time. Maybe it was jealousy. Maybe I felt rejected by my mother, that I was a burden to my father, so I had Lily. I had Lily to play with, to look out for, and to be in charge of, too. It made me feel in control of something. But I didn't even know where Lily was at the time, and after we left the trailer park and moved to the apartment, I would have none of those feelings.

I couldn't see her on the beach, although I was sure that's where she'd gone. It was just me and Krista and the blue heron. So

I was angry. Krista was on the log boom being a superhero, taller, braver, poised, calling me names, and I was on the beach, holding her clothes. But that was just what I expected, too, wasn't it?

"Don't fall," I called. It could have sounded like a warning, or a dare. She took it as a dare. She walked further out on the log boom. I looked to the heron, and just as I did, it extended its wings and flew off.

"Krista!" She waved me away with her hand and then put her fists on her hips, a Peter Pan stance to show me how sure of herself she was. I concentrated on her knees, imagined them shaking, then her feet, readjusting, but too suddenly so the rubber just slips on the wet log.

Then the wake reached the boom.

I had seen the tugboat coming, but so had Krista. I don't believe I knew any more than she did that this was the reason the heron had flown away, that although the tug was so quiet and the barge unassuming, the wake would hit a few minutes after they'd passed.

The log boom undulated and knocked above the waves and Krista's arms shot out straight. Her knees bent deeper. Then she lost her balance. Her weight went backwards, her feet slipped forward, and she fell between the logs.

At first I thought of the sturgeon. I wondered if Krista was saying her incantation under water, if she believed her own words now. I imagined the sturgeon swimming toward her, not as a vague shadow or a flash, but heavy, growing larger, Jurassic, its diamond back glowing brighter, mapping a trail to the other side, here to take her soul, but hitting its head on the log boom, just because she had said that, maybe, and I laughed. I laughed, not at Krista falling, at those other thoughts, and only because I didn't know what was about to happen. I hadn't seen Lily anywhere, but I hadn't looked for her, either. I didn't know she was just on the other side of one of those pilings, turning Barbie into a treeclimber and the horse into a Pegasus; that she had been watching Krista out on the log boom, too; that she'd heard everything I'd shouted, heard me tell Krista to fall; that she'd seen me laugh after she did; that she'd held her breath from the moment Krista went under until she could no longer hold it, and waited for minutes after that, not knowing what to do, or who to tell, because I was there. I was there and I'd seen what had happened and maybe I'd even made it happen, so she wondered, would telling someone about Krista mean telling someone about me? She was afraid I would be sent away. She was afraid of the things I would say to her. So don't tell anyone, I said, and we gathered Krista's clothes and threw them in the garbage. It's what I didn't say that made everything so much worse.

~

It wouldn't be the first time I'd had an abortion. The first time, I actually did ask Lily to come with me. I was still in high school and I didn't want anyone to look at me with contempt or pity, and I guess I was scared, too. She sat in the room with me. What a pair we were: me a pregnant teenager and her with that heavy eyeliner and clumped lashes, black stitches in her wrist, covered up, but not covered up, with a dozen black elastic bracelets. I lay on my back with a blue linen hospital gown on and the doctor, an old woman with a short perm, rolled a machine toward me, explained how she was going to insert a speculum, then the small plastic tube, and gentle suction.

"And then the anal probe?" Lily said with a nasal voice, which made me laugh, but also feel sick. "Sorry," she added.

But afterward, everything returned to normal. We kept our bedroom doors closed, snacked through dinner. I continued to ig-nore my dad's quiet taps on my door, pitiful "Good night." I put headphones on, turned up the volume just as Dad and Lily began talking in the room across the hall, and fell asleep to the same songs by Moist for over a year.

I opened the door. Lily wore white jeans, tight and tapered at the ankles, and a pale blue buttoned shirt. There wasn't a spot on them. She could be in a commercial for tampons, or anti-depressants, frolicking along some breezy ocean beach while a voice-over lists the side effects. She sliced her arm up so many times she could probably sew her own stitches. I wore a hooded sweatshirt, my short hair springing up with the static electricity.

"Come in," I said.

She glanced around, then sat down on the couch. I put the kettle on. I would have hot water, not coffee. I wanted to relax. I thought of Krista, in our trailer, grape juice with Dad and a smug face. "I need to talk to you," he'd said. Told me Krista had enough trouble at home without having to deal with nasty neighbours. "But she's older than me," I'd said. It made no sense. She had an empty plate in front of her, too, oily from cheese. I wondered how long she'd been there, having this private chat with my dad.

"It looks different in here," Lily said. The last time she was here, the couch arm was still intact. The beige carpet was disguised with a blue area rug, which I knew was odd—to put a rug over a rug—but everything was so brown when I moved in. Beige walls, beige carpet, yellow kitchen counter.

"I had that big acrylic on the wall over there. The ocean thing."

"Oh yeah—that thing was hilarious. What happened to that?"

It was garish, campy, with a tower of silvery fish schooling around itself, and tuna around those, dolphins around those. Above them, stars. "I threw it out."

"Oh." She smiled and crossed her legs, sitting up straight. How did a person like her end up with good posture?

I rinsed a mug out and waited by the element. The kettle was starting to heat up, making a sound like an empty shell. It was almost one o'clock. I could take a taxi to the clinic. That would be no problem.

"Dad's looking kind of thin these days," she said.

If I took a taxi home, though, they would wonder why no one

126

was picking me up. There would be concerned faces. I would be the oldest person there. Bad seed, I could tell them.

"Not in a good way," Lily added.

"He did just get hit by a car, right?" I poured my hot water, added a blast of lemon and leaned against the wall. Lily seemed to be waiting for me to say something else. "What?"

"He had to hire someone to help him cook and clean."

Did she want me to pity him? I hadn't thought of him as a father since we moved to the apartment. I assumed he'd given up on that idea, too. I sipped my water. Burnt my tongue.

"Do you realize it's been almost three years since we were all in the same room? And that was for his mom's funeral."

"Just how it goes, I guess." I wondered if people are just drawn to the ones that hurt them. All those years in the trailer, we were always in the same space, nothing but a vinyl curtain divid-ing us, but we moved to the apartment and we each had our own room. At first, it felt like a reward—compensation for having to move away. "I'm sorry you girls had to go through that," Dad said. He even cried about it, pulling us into him like a lifebuoy and kissing Lily on the neck.

Five to one. "I can't hang out for long, Lily. I have an appoint-ment I need to get to."

Lily took a mobile phone from her pocket. "We were talking about taking a trip—not anywhere too far. Dad knows this place that rents cob houses by a lake and you can fish there." She thumbed the screen. "I got a picture saved here. Just a second."

"Cob?"

Lily heaved a breath, impatient now. "He looks older since the accident."

I blew on my hot water, took a sip. Too much lemon. Dries out the mouth. "I'm not really into fishing." I couldn't imagine the three of us perched on a dock. I'd toss the worms in, let them sink. I had other things to think about. Inside me, it was only an embryo.

A potential. A question mark. I didn't want to know it.

Lily placed her phone on the arm of the couch and spun it around one way, then the other, like a combination lock.

"I'm not," I shrugged.

"Fine. You're not into fishing."

"Thank you." I sipped my water, but I could feel Lily looking at me. She pushed the phone away from her, a dramatic pause to get my attention. I remembered these looks at the apartment when I'd come out of my room to add macaroni to my boiling water or something. If she was watching TV, she'd turn it down. If she was looking for something in the fridge, she'd close the door and wait for me to finish. I never had anything to say, and neither did she.

"Aren't you tired of this?" she said.

"Of what?"

"Of this." She motioned toward me. "Being angry. If Dad can forgive us, I don't know why you're so mad at him."

"I don't want to talk about this with you," I said.

It was just as if Krista had disappeared. Her mother came home, asking around the park about her, angry at first. Then confused. Worried. Frantic. By the time the police came, she was all worn out, her face ruddy, dried up and tender like a sunburn. They found Krista's clothes in the garbage. A few days later, her body floated up downriver.

Dad had told us not to worry about Krista, but with a panic underneath. I wasn't worried about her. I was worried about being found out. So I left all those questions for the grown-ups to figure out, and they tried to do that by cutting into Krista, taking out her organs, her lungs full of water, maybe a bump on the head. They took a look at her uterus, too. So a dead pregnant twelve-year-old gave them another question.

After the police found her, it was quiet. Krista's mom sometimes came out of her stick and staple, wandered along the road in bare feet as though she was still looking for her. Lily and I stayed close to our trailer and played Go Fish. Krista's mom came over to us once, arms crossed with each hand holding the other elbow.

"You cared about my baby, didn't you?" she said.

"Do you have an eight?" I said to Lily.

Lily placed her hands on the table, making a wall with her cards. "Krista was our friend," Lily said without looking at her. "Daddy liked her, too." Krista's mom smiled, nodded.

"Lily, you have an eight." She scanned her cards, then tapped them into a single pile, spacing them out one by one, tedious. "Hurry up!" I said.

Krista's mom turned and wandered away. I wanted her to disappear, too. Soon she stopped wandering barefoot, but instead sat in her lawn chair smoking and watching Lily and me play. When Dad came home and kissed our heads, she watched that, too. When she got up, she was like a shark, wide-eyed and constant in her movement through the park, but with a long mint cigarette so we could almost smell her coming.

The police came back and talked to our neighbours again. They talked to Lily and me, too, but there was nothing to tell. They talked to Dad, long enough for everyone to look at us, for the old lady to stop giving us popsicles. The boy in the motorhome told us our dad was a "perv."

Lily was still looking at me, that pleading face. "Why do you hate him?"

"I don't hate him," I said. "I don't care enough for that." My lemon water was gone and I needed to call a cab soon.

Lily had one hand tangled up in her necklace. Was it a gift from Dad? I didn't want to know. "It's not like he meant to ignore us," she said. "He was just messed up."

"You think he ignored you?" I felt seasick. There was something inside me, a deep-down beat that was taking the silty nutrients from my veins. I closed my eyes and held my breath until my lungs felt like concrete and I wanted to vomit.

"I can't really blame him for it. If we'd told the truth, they probably wouldn't have done an autopsy."

"You think that would've been better?"

"What?"

I wrapped both hands around my mug even though it was empty. I never said anything about Krista. Never said anything about anything. "You think no one should've found out what happened to her?"

"No one did find out what happened!" Lily tugged pieces of foam from the couch and tossed them on the carpet like fish food. She stopped, stared at the carpet as if something was actually swimming up. "Why would you say that?"

"I don't know. I never knew for sure."

"Knew what?"

I needed to call a cab. I felt sick. It was time to go. "Never mind. It was so long ago." I walked over to the kitchen counter, but there was nothing I needed there.

"What was so long ago?" Lily demanded. "Just say it."

Did she want me to ask? I glanced at my jacket hanging on the door. There was the exit. It was hard to breathe in here, muggy, humid. Was the kettle boiling? I could just say it. I could just say it fast.

But it came out slowly. "What he did to Krista." I looked at Lily, waited for the flood I was sure would come.

She looked confused, as if trying to read something far away. "You think it was true," she said at last, horror spreading across her face. Her shoulders rose as she inhaled and stayed there.

I wanted to make her breathe again, or shout, cry—get it out. I wondered if it was all just too late, if she looked at this only as facts, forgives, forgets, at least for him. It was the only way to explain the visits, the caring—how she could still care. I didn't want to know, not really. I shook my head, but said, "What he did to you."

At first, she didn't move at all. She just stared at the bits of foam on the floor. After a moment, Lily laughed. She laughed so hard her body shook, and no sound came out. When she finally inhaled, she shouted to the ceiling, "Nothing like that ever happened!" She flung out her hands. "Why would you even say that?"

"I don't know. I don't know—because he would talk to you at night, those nights talking, I don't know." It felt like the ceiling was coming down. It was so muggy now. The air was heavy. I was sweating. The couch was soggy, waterlogged.

"Are you serious?" She put one hand on her mouth. She picked up her mobile phone, put it down again. It was so hot, my neck was clammy now. I would need a scarf to go outside.

She spoke to the wall opposite. "Talking."

I didn't say a word.

"The last time I got stitches, they made me wait three hours to tell a psychiatrist that I wasn't suicidal. I went home, told Dad I was moving out, and you know what he said? 'What about me?'" Lily looked at me, smiled as if this were a punchline. "We didn't talk," she said. "He just unloaded all his problems on me."

I thought of my dad, hair always too long over the ears. Home at six, then to bed for a nap. He never picked us up at school after we moved away. Never did anything with us.

"I have more reason to be angry than you," Lily said. "I should be mad at you! I was mad at you, but I got over that because you were a kid, too, and he was just a single dad with no friends and everyone looking at him like he was a pervert."

She was turning red, eyes pink and watery. "Now you tell me this? I have tried so hard to get you to visit him. It's like I'm the only person he has. You think that's been easy?" She looked small now with her face twisting up in that same clownish way it always did before crying, but she didn't cry, not really. She just became redder, damper, swollen. I wondered if this was how it felt inside me. If the amniotic fluid was heavier so it couldn't breathe right, if when I moved it felt like waves, if when I spoke, my words knocked above.

"And you thought that was happening and you just kept it inside?" Lily said.

I looked down into my mug. I couldn't get a breath. I brought the mug closer to my face, closer, and just tried to get a breath. Get a breath.

"What's the matter with you?"

I shook my head. Nothing. Nothing. "Nothing."

Lily moved toward me. I looked over to the door. Things around it began to dim. I could feel her, somewhere, moving toward me. The mug felt cold now and I dropped it in the sink.

I tried to get a breath. Ahead of me, the door.

Jane and the Whales

Ilsa Kyorkok, the hostess of the evening, is setting up the karaoke machine. Friday nights used to be for the drag queens to stride around the parquet dance floor, lip-syncing to jazz standards or pop divas, but they haven't been bringing the crowd like they used to, so the queens host karaoke instead. Ilsa places the machine on a table in the corner of the dance floor, untangling RCA cables, a power bar and patch cords, green sequined dress and long black wig, curly, sparkling pink lips, Egyptian eyes, the picture of an African queen, a goddess, Isis—yes! There's no such thing as overdressed!

Jane drapes her raincoat over a stool. She sits at the bar next to Matty, who wears the same red plaid jacket over a rainbow tie-dyed T-shirt as always, black jeans with a six-shooter belt buckle, and work boots, steel-toed although she is a web developer. "Look at you," Matty says, "Like something the tide brought in." She empties her pint.

"It's raining." Jane nods her head toward the little TV behind the bar, which always displays the weather channel. When she worked here, she'd leave it on the Food Network. With someone baking fennel and homemade tortellini in the background, those late, blurry nights almost felt good for her. But she wanted more light in her life, so she took a job selling organic cotton towels, beeswax candles, wooden flutes, Tibetan singing bowls. Recently, the manager ordered CDs with New Age, synthesized music and wolf howls or whale song, those songful moans of giant creatures calling to each other through the deep. Communication, navigation, or simply joy.

"It's so dead in here." Jane glances around the bar, nearly empty except for a few regulars. Ilsa Kyorkok lays two microphones on the table between coasters, so they don't roll away.

"It's early," Matty says.

"I thought karaoke would be a draw. Someone came to the store to give me a poster to put up." Jane taped the poster on the inside of the door. Behind the letters, a graphic of blue and white swirled together.

"Did you?" Matty says.

"Of course." Jane took the news of Karaoke Night as a sign, and when she looked up, the store didn't seem so full of light any-more, but walled in with card racks and towels and tapestries that deadened the acoustics. It felt like she was in a sea of fine saw dust. She recalled all those times when singing transported her some-where, when she literally left her body behind for a while as she flew through the air, over the city. At first she didn't know what was happening, but soon came to expect this transcendental experi-ence. But all those times she had flown from her body, she always ended up at the The Blue Room, wondering why. This poster was meant for her. This time, she would begin the journey at The Blue Room, sing there, leave from there. Maybe she would find the an-swers in her next destination.

Matty calls the bartender, Ned, over for another. He stops digging high ball straws out of the drain to help her, then hands her a coaster.

"What the hell is this for?" Matty waves the coaster.

Ned shrugs, smiling, and returns to the sink.

"First the fucking hand sanitizer and now coasters," Matty shakes her head. "What's next—dress codes?" she calls over to Ned. The bathrooms were redone last month with larger toilet paper reels. The coasters are supposed to protect the bar, which is still shit, the varnished chipped away by absent-minded fingernails. The low pan-elled ceiling, spray painted black with glow-in-the-dark stars stuck to it, is going to be redone, too. The stars were put up fifteen years ago, ambitiously, at the same time as the silver glitter Mac-tack on the pil-lars. Most of the stars have fallen down, so they look like mistakes now.

"That's going to a stone tile," Ned says. "The new owners are going to redo all of it, expand the crowd in here. The bar's not making money like it used to."

"But if they 'expand the crowd,' then it won't be a gay bar, really."

Ned shrugs. "I don't know, Jane," he says, and places a pint in front of her.

"So you're actually here for the karaoke?" Matty says, turning toward Jane on her stool.

"I'm going to sing. Maybe. I haven't decided." Jane needs time to find a song that will work. Something melodious and high, something with pure vowels she can ride into the sky. It's only when the overtones really ring out that she lifts out of her body.

"What's to decide? It's just fucking karaoke. And it's dead, anyway. Wait a minute—are you dolled up?"

Matty smirks at Jane's red polka-dot blouse, jeans and black lace-up boots, which she chose to offset the feminine ruffles. Dangling in the blouse's V-neckline is a red and yellow jade pendant with two fish. At first glance, someone might think she was Chinese with this pendant, her olive skin and wide nose, but they would be confused by her strawberry blonde hair, shaped into loose curls to her shoulder. "What are you?" she was often asked by strangers when she bartended. "A bartender," she'd respond with a tight smile.

"This old thing?" Jane jokes.

"You wanna get laid," Matty teases.

"That's not why I'm here."

"Oh God, I don't mean me, miss virgin. It's too fucking quiet in here, anyway."

Matty is usually at the pool table, but there's no one around to play. Except for Richard, but he's always here. Looks like he could use a meal or two, wilting in the corner by the fire exit, grey-brown hair and a nose as narrow as the rest of him. And that boy, Aaron, with one of his straight girlfriends. What's her name again? Samantha? Sarah? Samantha, maybe. Aaron's hair is bleach-blonde this week, his T-shirt is pink, and he's piled on the bangles. The effect might be festive if the bangles weren't gold and copper-coloured.

They remind Jane of a bellydancer. Samantha is wearing black and white high-heeled boots and a sparkling butterfly barrette that holds one straightened lock off her forehead. The KENO board glitters behind them.

"Just a few more minutes!" Ilsa Kyorkok shouts, holding up the binder of song choices.

"What are you singing, Jane?" Matty says.

"I don't know yet. I need to really think about it. It has to be a perfect song." Jane's beer tastes flat and metallic. The draught here is terrible. She puts it on the coaster and turns to Matty. "Remember when I told you about the astral projections?"

"I musta been too drunk. Refresh me."

Jane tucks a piece of blonde hair behind her ear and leans her head on her fist. "Okay, well, it started when I was in high school. In choir." It was a secular school, and choir was open to anyone, no audition necessary, but almost all the repertoire was on a Christian theme. There were nineteenth-century lullabies with sopranos matched up to altos, and tenors and basses that moved along parallel with each other. There were largo Latin pieces with four-part harmonies, each taking its turn leaping up as one line swells or overtakes the others with a high pitch on a wide open vowel, like "oh." Jane liked to sing "oh." "Ah" was too wide open, difficult to focus the sound so that she ran out of breath quickly, and she was never sure how much to round her lips.

She also liked "ee"; the sound always found its way to some space between her eyes, resonating there so that her whole head vibrated like a hammered bell. So she liked the Latin pieces the best, *no-o-o-n nobis do-o-o-mine non no-o-o-b-i-i-i-s*. She wished there was a song where the sopranos could just sing those vowels way up high on one note the whole way, way up high and stay there, their heads ringing in unison on their side of the choir bleachers. She imagined jumping up out of the sound to an even higher note, climbing up the scale of overtones, first the fundamental harmonic, then the second, then the third, like a band of white light fanning into colour, something so beautiful that everyone listening raises their chins, a mimetic impulse to lift themselves up, up, up.

It was a natural progression from the oh's and ee's to the om. Jane would sit cross-legged on her bedroom floor with each hand on one knee, palms turned upward, fingers cupped slightly, sensing the bowl of energy in each one. O-o-o-o-m-m-m. O-o-o-o-m-m-m. She let her mind wander. The giggling guru lisping his way through an interview, marigold necklace, marigolds floating on a muddy lake (or is it the Ganges?), funeral pyre, campfire, black marshmallows, bathing suit, the Saan Clothing Store ...

Richard is trying to order a gin and tonic at the other end of the bar. Ned grabs a high ball glass and fires ginger ale into it then turns his back to Richard for a moment before popping two straws in, no gin. "On the house." Richard takes the drink and shuffles back to his table. It's a miracle he doesn't spill.

"That is a miracle," Jane agrees.

"Sorry," Matty says. "I interrupted you."

"That's all right. I was about to tell you about flying."

Jane would focus the om so her sinus cavity vibrated and her eyes became watery in their sockets, overtones whistling through her nose. When she opened her eyes, she was looking down at herself, at the top of her head, palms still resting on her knees. She looked toward the window and imagined flying clear out of the room, maybe to Nepal, or the middle of the Arctic Ocean, or the Indian Ocean, diving down. These were the places she thought she would go. But she could not control her mind.

So she was above the Saan now, floating past the seagull standing on the edge of the roof, overlooking two kids leaning against the brick trading off a cigarette, over the houses, mossy asphalt shingles and droopy wood siding, sweaty paned glass windows, bare trees slick and black. Then the view turned from A-line rooftops to flat, square tops with a few aluminum pipes sticking out, re-bars, playgrounds obscured by black branches, then dimming light, to parking lots wide open, the white painted lines like chalk on a blackboard, vehicles marking the lot like exes and oh's, copper-topped older buildings made up of stone blocks, brick ones falling down and red dragons round the lampposts, when she started to descend like a tired helium balloon. Her feet touched the pavement at last and she stood outside a black door, matte and scratched, black and white circles of old gum and bird shit around her feet. Jane opened the door, and followed a rail down wooden stairs, worn blonde in the centre. And that is how Jane first came to this bar. It was called Rumors then.

~

"And then what happened?" Matty says.

"What do you mean? That's it."

"That's your story? What happens at the bar?"

"I don't know. The usual, I guess. That's the problem."

"I think you're just changing the subject," Matty says. "So what are you gonna sing?"

"I don't know if I'm changing the subject. I'm trying to get to the bottom of it."

Matty nods, drums a syncopated rhythm on the bar, nodding to inaudible rock, staring at the weather channel.

Jane wonders what she is listening to. "Have you ever flown like that?"

"What's that—astral projection? Of course I know what that is. The seventies. I was there, remember?" Matty pinches her tie-dyed shirt, offering it as proof of her knowledge of transcendental philosophy.

"So you haven't flown," Jane adds.

Matty scratches the seam of her jeans. "Do you mean literally fly? Or, like, in my mind?"

"Both."

"Where would I go?"

"I don't know. That's the point. You go somewhere, but then you have to figure out why. That's what I can't figure out. Why I always ended up at this bar. But now I wonder if this was just a rest-stop."

Matty glances at the TV near the cash register. The weather channel is reporting the expected precipitation for the night and high winds. "Okay. I got a flying story. It happened one summer on this little Gulf Island where we used to camp when I was a kid. There was this big wharf."

The wharf went out far enough for the water taxis to deliver passengers even at low tide, which they did at the lower dock, which was connected to the end of the wharf by a ramp. Even at high tide, the drop from the end of the wharf was high enough to experience some thrill of free-falling, and at low tide, this was even more extreme.

"Or so I'd heard, right. 'Cause all those years of visiting that place—hanging around the wharf where all those teenaged boys were catching mud sharks, laying 'em out to shrivel up on the dock, then taking turns leaping off the end of the wharf, arms and legs waving all over the place—well, I never had the guts to do it." Matty takes a sip of beer. "Until the summer I turned thirteen."

Matty was playing on the lower dock, catching shiners that swam around the pilings to deliver to the older boys for mud shark bait, which they were usually grateful for. "They'd say, 'Thanks Matty,' and I thought, Hey, I like that—Matty, 'cause my folks would never call me that. So I was one of the guys—the little guy. But this one day, I gave them my catch, and when I turned to go back to the lower dock, one of the boys said, "Hey Matilda, your bathing suit is up your butt.'"

Matty had twisted around to face them and plucked her swimsuit out of her butt, which was definitely up it. The other

139

boys laughed and Matty realized at that moment that she was not a kid anymore, nor was she the little guy. She was old enough now to pick on. So she stopped catching shiners for them and instead hung out on the wharf eating sunflower seeds, reading Archie comics, and trying to stay out of sight. When the boys had gone, she stood at the edge of the wharf, looking down at the dark green ocean and trying to calm the butterflies in her stomach. This went on for several days. Then one day, three older girls, late teens or even twenties, disembarked from the water taxi below, carrying canvas backpacks and wearing short white shorts and halter tops, all of them tanned, sungoddess kind of stuff. They climbed the ramp, one of them lighting a cigarette as she did so, then immediately dumped their bags in the middle of the wharf. After the other taxi passengers had gone, the one with the cigarette butted it on the dock, took her top off and dropped her shorts, revealing a green terry cloth bikini underneath, very sixties, ran toward the end of the wharf and flew off.

"It was the first time I'd seen a woman jump before. They looked so cool, I thought 'I want to be like them.' Maybe I could, you know?" So after all the women had jumped in, Matty approached the edge, arms folded across her chest. The women treaded water below, their long hair fanning out behind them, slippery legs beating, breasts all floating and luscious. Matty thought of her suit up her butt, imagined being down there with them, how she could never look like that, how inadequate, how the boys would say something nasty if they saw her there, compare them, and she was almost about to leave when the woman in the terry cloth suit called up at her, "Jump! Jump! Jump!" until they were all chanting. But it was not like taunting. With their long hair and tanned bodies and bikinis, Matty imagined they were cheerleaders, sent here from the heavens to help her jump. She wanted so badly to do it, but not because she wanted to be like them.

"You know what I'm talking about," Matty nudges Jane. "So I took a breath, butterflies going crazy in my gut, the wind picked up, ocean got darker—deep looking." Matty points at the TV, which displays video of dark clouds gathering over the downtown harbour. "Ominous. Ocean got so dark, I couldn't even see their legs anymore. I could see something though, like giant fish, maybe kelp, but maybe not." Just as Matty had wondered, *Wait—are those tails? Are they dangerous?*—it was too late because she had already taken a single step forward and was falling, falling, falling, and then everything was quiet and cold, and her arms were floating out to the sides, and she was weightless, flying. She opened her eyes under water to see where she was, and was surprised the saltwater did not hurt. And all around was the dark green and the woman with the terry cloth bikini smiled at her and her long hair waved upwards like eel grass, and the other women made a circle around Matty, locking hands and smiling, teeth glinting like mirrors in the water. They were all weightless and flying, soaring underwater and Matty explored below the lower dock and saw a perch look up at her sideways, and caught a shiner in her hand, and chased mud sharks away. And when she at last surfaced again, into the golden, blinding sun, the boys had returned to the dock and the women were nowhere to be seen. Not even the cigarette butt.

"Is that true?" Jane asks.

"It is true," Matty says. "Sure as hell."

Jane recalls the books at the store she's browsed on quiet days, shamans and spirit guides, and transformative flashes of light. "Do you think they were helping spirits?"

"If that's what you wanna call smokin' hot women, sure." Matty grins.

Jane takes her coaster and taps it as she talks. "But you said they mysteriously disappeared or something, so they must have been spirit guides, or some kind of spiritual entity."

"Are you getting annoyed?"

"No! I just—" Jane lays the coaster down again. "Fine. They were hot women."

"Exactly," Matty says, and takes a sip of beer. "I turned into a stud that day."

Jane waits for Matty to elaborate, but she just winks, and turns to the hostess, Ilsa Kyorkok. Ilsa tugs her panty hose up, from the ankle, then shin, knee. The other TVs around the room flash on and silhouetted gogo dancers rock their hips to the tinny music that rattles through the bar. Then the screen goes blue, and Ilsa Kyorkok snaps her fingers into the microphone.

"Okay, people. Don't everyone sign up at once. You!" She points to Aaron and his friend, Samantha. "You got something you wanna sing? Or do you need me to warm us up?" Ilsa wags her tongue at the mic before snapping back, laughing low and rumbling. "Okay, here goes." She puckers her lips and sways, one finger-nailed hand on her waist. Plodding piano, pop music of the seventies.

"This song always sounded Jesus-y to me," Matty says.

"What is it?"

"Oh God, you're a baby. 'You Light Up my Life.' Debby Boone."

"Right. I know it. It's about God?"

"I don't know. I'm just saying it sounds like something God-people would make about God."

A flute trickles down, and the horns murmur below. Ilsa sings about light and hope, punctuating the ends of each phrase with a flip of her hair and a tongue across her upper teeth, squinting at the TV as if she is reading a chart in an eye exam.

Jane first saw Ilsa Kyorkok lip-syncing "Midnight Train to Georgia." Her black curls were wrapped up in a pink scarf and the way she rocked in her pink jumpsuit, she really did look like Gladys Knight. But Ilsa's real singing voice was nothing like Knight's syrupy gospel. Ilsa sounds more like Bob Dylan, wavering in the treble despite her low speaking voice. Jane thinks of a jaw harp. Then a banjo, a porch in the Appalachia, Ilsa leaning in the cabin doorway in her green sequined dress. That looks dangerous, she thinks, and turns to Ilsa, relieved she is here instead.

"Jesus. I can't listen to her sing all night," Matty says. "Maybe we should do one." She leans over the bar and takes a pen from a mug.

"What's that for?" Jane says.

"My request." Matty writes, 'Like a Virgin' on a napkin, then pushes it to Jane. "You sing this, I'll buy you another beer."

"Everyone does "Like a Virgin.""

"Everyone? Really. Look around Jane. It's dead."

"I don't want to sing that. Besides, you can't just write a song on a napkin—you have to look it up in the binder. And I don't know what I want to sing yet, if they even have a song that will work—"

"All right, simmer down. You're like a teenager sometimes, you know that?" Matty moves the napkin aside. "It's just fucking karaoke, Jane."

That's not why we're here, though, that's just where we are, right? "It's got to be more than that. It's got to be more than just getting drunk, and dancing, and singing."

"I don't know why that's not enough for you, Jane. That sounds pretty good to me. We're like a bunch of fucking shamans in here." Matty raises her glass in a toast.

Jane clinks her beer, but she is not convinced. "It's not just what we do, it's how it feels when we do it."

Matty takes the napkin and places it beside her coaster. "You think too much, Jane."

But her mind is free, isn't it? "One day, I astral travelled completely by accident," she tells Matty.

～

A few years after Jane graduated from high school, she joined a community choir. The choir director was in a sparkling mood, telling jokes with his eyes getting wider each time they met with laughter. "To hell with the sheet music. Today we're doing something completely different." He would improvise. He signed the notes to each section. "The basses, do. The tenors, mi. Altos, so. Sopranos ... . ready ... Do. Hold, hold, hold. Now sopranos ..." Rise dreamily to the major ninth. "Re." His hands moved the sound step by step, morphing harmonies from minor sevenths to major sixes, nines, twelves, to sound clusters, pentatonic blurs, then the sopranos moved steadily upwards, a ladder, mi ... fa ... so ... . then the director's shoulders rise, his chin lifts, ready ... "do!" And Jane is up. Jane is flying through the halo up through the ceiling, up, into the clouds, disoriented, spinning, head ringing when the sound decrescendos, tick, tock, down, through the gauzy clouds, wipes them from her face like spiders' silk, opens her eyes, which felt like cotton, down. And here again in the city. But she couldn't even tell what year it was. Projections span distance and time, and you can't tell what you're looking at, like a quasar, an ancient galaxy whose light has only just reached the orbiting camera, whose light has travelled so far, in fact, that what you see is the light that left the quasar fifteen billion years ago. That what you see is the past, before any of this even happened.

～๑

"What did the place look like?" Matty says.

"The carpet was spongy. The tables were spongy, too, sort of diapered in red terry cloth."

"Sounds like the beer parlour days, seventies maybe. Was I there?"

"I don't know. I only flew a few times." Jane had imagined these flights would reveal the world to be an expansive place, various, or connect her to someone far away, maybe, or something godly. Why not whales? She was always drawn to whales, and the image of a blue whale diving deep down in the middle of the Indian Ocean, down where it's cool where the krill live, where she could follow them, keep up just enough to not lose sight of their blue bodies in the deep. But she always just arrived at the bar. Believing her destination was predictable, and seeing only a bar, her mind was no longer open to possibility. So that was the last time she flew.

After a couple of years, she wanted to find the bar again. Partly because she was curious if it really existed, if all the flights had actually happened, and partly because she was a homo, and she wanted to be around other homos.

Matty laughs. "There ya go, Jane."

"But was there something more to this?"

"Why do you need more?" Matty says. "You remind me of my niece—'How big is the universe? How can a number go on forever? How do I know I'm here and not just imagining this?' But she was ten for that phase."

Just as she says this, two women in jean skirts enter the bar, collapsing umbrellas. Jane thinks they look like the sailors' wives, out for a girls' night on the town, to The Blue Room so their husbands won't have to be jealous.

"That's funny," Matty says. "What would you guess about me?"

"I'm not guessing," Jane says. "Those women have been here before. When I bartended, I got to know everyone." It is hard to see the mystical in something so familiar.

That's what happened with the community choir. "One night after the Christmas concert, I went out with a handful of choir members for drinks to the Irish pub. It was the first time I'd hung out with anyone, outside of rehearsals." Ron, a tenor, had two small children and, boy, is choir practice a welcome break. Lisa, an alto, was in an amateur production of *Hello, Dolly!* and was going to go to RADA, but what are the odds of success? What a crapshoot. That's true, isn't it? says Marianne, another alto. Did you know Laura and Robbie are dating? Another round. Who else? I think I've seen some eyes between Zoe and Jason, Ron says. What about Ted? I don't know, says Lisa. I think he's probably gay. Don't say that, says Marianne. Oh God, Marianne. You're in the stone age. Another round.

"After that, I watched the faces in choir as much as the director.

I milled around with my Styrofoam cup of coffee during the break, watching eyes. The nights felt late. By the end of practice, my feet were sore from standing, and then choir was just a chore."

"That makes no sense," Matty says. "You're too fucking sensitive. People are people."

"But it wasn't about music anymore—it wasn't about celebration."

"Maybe that stuff was all you guys had in common."

"No—what about the music?"

"Oh God, Jane, you can't spend a whole night talking about 'Ave Maria' or some shit."

The sailors' wives, seeing that the bar is empty, clop up the stairs again, into the rain.

Ilsa is nearly finished now. "You light up my life, baby!" Matty shouts.

Ilsa turns to her, one hand on her narrow hip. "You just committed to a song."

"I got it here!" Matty waves the napkin at Ilsa, but she is making the next selection, and hands the mic to Richard, who says, "You shoulda been a beauty queen."

"I am a beauty queen," Ilsa says. Richard leans one hand on the table and a synthesized orchestra swells. The words appear on the TV and he bellows his best Sinatra with the opening lines to "My Way." He pushes off the table so he is upright, but now leans precariously the other way. Ilsa shuffles with bent knees on the tops of her heels to retrieve Richard a chair.

Aaron and Samantha drink rum and cokes and continue to look through the binder, with periodic outbursts of laughter, at which point Aaron shouts, "Not laughing at you, Richard! You're doing awesome."

The first time Matty came here, she swam, head full of peach schnapps, if you can believe it, eyes like fish in a tank. Took one look around this place, thought, "Hallelujah, I'm home."

"Still remember the song—it was that Donna Summer song, wanna share my love with a wo-man lover, da, da, da ... you know it. And I thought, fucking eh, right."

Matty taps her finger on the bar, humming through the rest of the song. "Right. 'Hot Stuff.' That one."

Ned drops another coaster in front of Matty. "She says 'warm-blooded lover,' actually," he says.

"What? Bull."

"She's a born-again Bible-thumper."

Matty places her glass on the coaster. "Warm-blooded, eh? Well, doesn't matter. I'm still gonna sing wo-man."

Jane picks absent-mindedly at the hem of her blouse, then holds the fish pendant in her hands. "I got this at the store for a discount," she says, and lets it drop to her chest again.

"Don't be bummed out, Jane." Matty says. "Look—you got nearly a full beer, good company, it's fucking pissing outside and it's dry in here. Just enjoy yourself."

Matty was right about the rain. The weather channel is scrolling text along the top of the TV about a wind warning, and heavy rain. "It's just weather," Jane says.

"Oh God. You know Michael got struck by lightning once, eh?" Matty nods toward Ilsa.

"What? No." Jane must've made a hundred mudslides for Ilsa.

"Then I got a story for you."

Before Ilsa Kyorkok was Ilsa Kyorkok, she was just plain Michael. Michael was a bluegrass fan, probably the only black bluegrass fan in all of Alberta, but he was usually the only black everything where he grew up, so he tried to be honest with himself about what he was really authentically drawn to so when he was a teenager, he thought it was bluegrass. He wore Wrangler jeans and brown cowboy boots to the folk house concerts, but never a cowboy hat. He wore a ball cap instead, not wanting to stand out more than he already did, not wanting to be too tall in the crowd. At home, he practised strumming his Gibson guitar, C, F, G, C, plucking the bass note with his thumb between each downward stroke, and sing- ing in his room about Tennessee mountains and corn whisky. His mother never had to ask him to keep it down, because Michael was shy, even at home, and kept his singing almost to a whisper. She didn't like his taste in music, but knew that boys his age often go through phases, and if she complained about this, he would prob- ably just love it even more.

One day, his mother took him to the annual Bluegrass Festival that was held up at the little ski hill in the summer. It was a small festival, with the big stage at one end, and the smaller chuckwagon stage at the other for the local acts. Near this stage, vendors laid out their wares on card tables—T-shirts, ball caps, belt buckles, jew- elry, hotdogs, hamburgers, and burritos. And the grassy expanse between was checked with picnic blankets and music lovers in cow- boy hats and sundresses.

Michael and his mother took their picnic blanket and found a patch of grass a little up the ski hill with an excellent view of the main stage, and not too close to people. His mother did not like crowds.

"Can't say I'm too comfortable with them either sometimes, if you know what I mean," Matty says, making a fist.

Singer-songwriters, four-piece bands, and trios took turns on the main stage all afternoon. Michael was thrilled to hear the claw- hammer banjo picking and the fiddler ripping between verses and soaring up to the choruses. The way it came on so suddenly, it was almost as if the fiddler had evoked the storm. Dark grey-blue clouds gathered at the top of the hill, then over the main stage. The vendors began stuffing their T-shirts and jewelry into duffle bags as the rain started to drizzle. Then the loudest thunder bellowed through the dark sky, and the musicians stopped playing, moved their instruments into the dry corners and abandoned the stage. The festival-goers collected their blankets and darted for their vehicles. At first, Michael and his mother had the idea to huddle up under the pine tree nearby, hoping the rain would pass quickly. But then a sudden flash illuminated the lawns, transforming the wet grass into silver blades. They started to dash for the car, running through the middle of the field, his mother holding the blanket over her head to protect her hair from the rain, when Michael was suddenly stopped.

In a single moment, the world lit up around him, flashed silver and remained there, illuminated. It was as if he'd been living in strobe light until this moment, unable to see the whole picture, unable to see the way one moment travelled fluidly to the next, and now, in this frozen flash, he saw it all: his whispered singing; his mother's worry about crowds, so much worry that even in an emergency, she prefers to flee alone; his ball caps because what would happen if he wore a cowboy hat, a sky-high black one with a silver buckled band and a black shirt with pearl buttons and ruby-red roses embroidered above the front pockets, and then, Oh! What a force! Electric! Fabulous! He would not have to be so quiet. Then the thunder crashed again and Michael was out. Out like a light.

He woke later in the hospital. His mother had resuscitated him. He developed cataracts and had to get surgery to see right again. But he says he never saw anything the same. Because his personality changed, too.

"That sometimes happens with lightning strikes," Matty says.

"Wait," Jane says, "I feel like you missed a beat. You mean a lightning strike turned him into a drag queen?"

"Hell, no. Michael was always a queen. He was just going through a bluegrass phase. It was the lightning that took away his shyness. Shy people are always thinking frame to frame, so it's hard for them to go with the flow. Like me. See?" Matty holds up her beer and smiles. "Flow," she says, then drinks to the bottom of the glass.

"That's it?" Jane says. "He's touched by God in a flash of light and becomes outgoing?"

"You sound disappointed, Jane." Matty tilts her head thought-fully, her mouth half-smiling in a tiny smirk.

"Well, it just seems a little trivial, don't you think? If I was struck by lightning and almost died and had to be resuscitated, I hope I would get more out of it than that."

Matty shakes her head and turns to her beer again. "I don't know what you want from me, Jane. If you can't see what a fucking gift that was, then I don't know what to tell you."

Jane stares at the crow's feet around Matty's eyes. There is one long silver hair growing in her eyebrow. She is much older than Jane. Matty is right; she doesn't know what Jane wants. Jane wants ... Jane wants ... More. She wants more from this beer, this coaster, that story, this bar. Everything! she wants to shout. Everything!

Richard hands the microphone to Ilsa and goes back to his table in the far corner. He hunches over the table, tearing up a napkin, and places the pieces deliberately around his glass of ginger ale.

"Your turn, cowboy," Ilsa says, handing Aaron the mic. He slides his voice up and down searching for the pitch so he misses the first line, finds his spot for the next one, "Finally," that nineties disco anthem.

"This song reminds me of a party I went to at the United Church hall when I was a teenager," Jane says.

"Church party, eh?" Matty says, and pretends to fall asleep.

Jane wonders if she takes anything seriously. "It was some kind of Christian rave." Jane had found a flyer on the only unoccupied table in a café, and thought, of all the tables, this is the one that is left for me. The lights came from the DJ's side of the room, pink, red, purple lights shifting to yellows and oranges, and back like a sunset, light particles wrapping around channels of sound and moving through the crowd like a hand through water. The kids, most of them teenagers, hopped nearly in unison, their arms waving above them in the dense humidity, some with whistles bursting in syncopation with the beat, then, when the beat stopped and only the shimmering synthesized sound kept going, the strobe light began indicating the moment to slow down, see it frame by frame by frame—"Look! Look at what is happening here!" A female voice sang, "He is the way, the truth, and the life. No one comes to the Father except through him."

Before this voice, Jane was one molecule of the same water. Before this voice, she believed she'd found her destination. But the words did not make sense to her. She did not like to imagine a gate-keeper to grace. She brought this up outside, where a few people were smoking. "I'm just here to make fun of it," one girl laughed and the two boys laughed with her.

"Yeah, sometimes we gotta travel around a bit to find our peo-ple. Just be happy you found us when you did," Matty says as Ned brings her another beer. "Holy, foam!" she says, but Ned points to his ear, shaking his head, and smiling. Matty shrugs, raises her pint, "Here's to foam." When she brings the glass down, she has foam along her top lip. "Does the body good," she says, pointing.

"I guess so," Jane says.

"You don't sound convinced." Matty wipes the foam away with her hand, as if smoothing out a moustache. "Probably don't know Richard's story either, eh?"

Jane glances at Richard, who is hunched over his table, nod-ding. "He doesn't talk much."

"You always got the late shifts, I guess," Matty says. "Gotta catch him earlier in the day."

Long before Richard was just Richard at the bar, he was a log-ger. One day, on his hike out of the bush, he stepped onto a fallen fir and slipped because the bark was loose, falling backwards. Although he did not see it as he fell, waiting for him below was the stump of a balsam tree that had been cut at a sharp angle. When the tree fell, it left one narrow spire, and this is what Richard fell on, piercing his side. So he was no longer able to work, but was left to recover in a downtown hotel room in the city, collecting Workers' Compensation, and lucky to be alive.

He stayed in his cot all day, staring out his small window at the grey cityscape, and only two fuzzy channels on the old TV in his room kept him company. He became bored, and felt useless, and his muscles diminished with a poor diet of minute rice and cup-a-soups, and he began drinking more, fireball whisky and sometimes rum, which was sweet and made him feel sticky, so he smoked more and more to dry himself out, but as he dried out, he only became more thirsty. But still, he diminished, like a puddle in the sun, until he was like a cracked, clay depression on the ground. His skin became delicate. So delicate, that as he lay in bed one day, absent-mindedly scratching an itch on one elbow, his nails began to click against himself, and when he looked, he saw that he had scratched right through the skin to the white bone, not smooth and slippery, but dry as sandpaper. He stopped washing himself, afraid his skin would all wash away, mud down the drain, and he would be left with only a tired skeleton. He drank more to stop himself from turning to dust completely.

When the fireball and the rum could no longer keep the thirst at bay, Richard wandered the streets outside, looking for a new drink. He knew about this place; it had been there for years, and by the time the eighties happened, the bar was common knowledge to most anyone living in the city. The bar had the same look as the strung-out faces that teetered along the sidewalks and collapsed in doorways. Fuck it. Fucking faggots, he thought. He returned to his room, passed out in his cot, slept until three, hair of the dog, black and white TV. They had cable back at the logging camp, thank jesus fucking christ. Amen. But who knows if he'd get back there again. That was '85. Look at me, he thought. Fucking loser. Forty fucking years old and look at this fucking room. I need a drink. I need a drink, I neeeeeed a long, long drink.

He drank every drop and went outside again. Stumbled down the stairs to The Blue Room, but it was called Fanfare then. The music thudded inside. Then this young guy says, "I know you.

Remember me?" he says. "Mr. Logger-man, stud, you remember me, right?"

Yeah, I do. Richard nods. He always ended up downtown like this, even before the fall, before, when he still had big muscles and knew how to wield a chainsaw six hours a day. Before, when he stumbled through the night all muddy and crashed into someone outside once in a while.

So he kept coming back and he changed his drink. Highballs. G&Ts and rum and cokes, and the bar was so humid on those nights when it filled up with young men with moustaches who took their shirts off when they danced, and pulled them through their belt loops for safekeeping; old men who sat at the bar in jean jackets even though it was too hot for that. Richard kept his plaid shirt buttoned at the wrist so no one would see the bone protruding, and the humidity kept his thirst at bay. After a while, the skin grew back. Eventually, Richard sat at the bar with the other men, and sometimes, Richard danced, too.

Jane glances over at Richard, who has organized his napkin scraps into two piles. He scratches his cheek as he stares, deep in concentration.

"Richard still drinks like a fish," Jane says.

"Sure, but he's not all bone. That's the point, Jane. He was gonna fall right off his bones. Not everything gets solved in one go."

"But what's he thirsty for now?"

"Same as you, maybe. Lately, he's always on about reading tea leaves and seeing the future or something. But he won't drink tea, so he tears up fucking napkins and spreads 'em around the table all night. He's a one-of-a-kind, anyway."

Aaron has abandoned the words and improvises to "oo." Even Ilsa has stopped dancing, and leans against the wall waiting for the song to end.

"Then we're always thirsty," Jane says. "Is that it?"

Matty doesn't hear this question. "Jane, please sing something, these kids are killing me."

"No. I don't know what to sing yet. I need to think about this."
This can't be it. She can't sing "My Way," or "Like a Virgin," all
these other people's songs, their words in her mouth, words that
sell records, and that's all, isn't it? Reading the words off a TV. No.
The music has to come from deep down, the pure vowels, for it to
work. And if she can do it here, from The Blue Room, maybe she
will find her true destination, if there is a next destination. If there
is anything to this at all.

"Just pick one or I'll pick for you."

If Matty tells Michael, she will pressure Jane to sing. She will
be sassy and loud, and next to the sequined dress and the curly
wig and the booming voice through glittered lips, "My Way" and
"Finally," and "You Light Up My Life," it would be ridiculous to
refuse. Matty will look at her, call her a teenager again, miss virgin.
"I know you sing," she'll say. "We know you're not Maria Callas,
honey," Ilsa will coax. I know, I know, Jane will say. That's not it.
So what is it then? Just sing! It's just fucking karaoke. Why won't
you sing something for us? The bar fridge hum is getting louder.
Ned turns on the tap, which whirs like a tiny spring vibrating on
the head of a pin.

"Please don't pick one for me," Jane says.

"Then you better get up there."

"Sing your own fucking song!"

Matty's laugh begins with one burst, "Ha!" then settles in-
ward, inaudible, just convulsing shoulders and a shaking head, as
if she is always tsk-tsking the things that make her laugh. "Relax!
Have another drink." Matty shakes her head as she brings her glass
up to her lips, then stops shaking to drink. Jane nudges the bottom
of her glass, spilling beer down the sides of Matty's face, dribbling
onto her chest.

"Fuck, Jane!"

"Oh my God, sorry!" Jane sucks her lips in to control a smile.

Matty holds her arms out, surveying the spill. "Get me a fuckin' towel or something." Matty does not look angry. She looks as if she's been told a bigoted joke, too stupid for words. She looks disappointed. Jane should have clapped for Ilsa more, for Richard. She'll clap for Aaron—she'll whistle with her teeth.

"I'm sorry," Jane says.

"Forget it."

What would she have done in the bar with the terry-clothed tables if she had not simply flown away? When the longshoreman elbowed the woman's drink off the bar, muttered, "Fuckin' queer," and the woman jumped back to avoid the spill, held her arms up to survey the damage, then shoved him off his stool. The bar was tired of fights, flying bottles and tipped tables, so they threw her out after only a few punches, after only her bloody nose and his bruised rib. The man downed his beer and left, too. Two men followed, and other women ran out after, the sound of chairs knocking into tables as they shoved past them like a herd of furious elephants.

Ned hands Matty a clean white towel.

"Now it's as wet in here as it is out there," Matty says, nodding her chin toward the weather channel, which issues wind warnings. The cloud icon has become darker, and the rain heavier, but they can't hear any of that from down here.

"I'm sorry." Jane goes to the bathroom.

The stalls have new doors already, clean and white. Not like the black ones that used to be here with bits of glue from stickers and engraved messages, some old, some new, "I love pussy." A timeless sentiment. "Womyn warriors unite!" Early nineties, perhaps? "Carla is a liar!!!" An angry ex. But that is all gone. The doors are a blank slate. Jane feels her pockets for something sharp. A bobby pin she could take the rubber tip off. What would she write? What should be here? Maybe "Jane was here." Too generic. "Jane is here. Why? Be Here Now. Pick a song." She scrapes into the door, Is this it?

Jane washes her face and dabs it dry with toilet paper. She doesn't want to get attention like that. Outside, she hears a woman's voice now, singing about making it through the wilderness. Then Ilsa. There is a break in the singing, but the music plods onward. Matty is laughing. Ilsa picks up the next line, too.

Jane closes her eyes and quietly joins in on the next line. On "blue," the oo bounces around the bathroom tile and veneered counter tops, aluminum, ceramic bowls. She tries the next line an octave higher, imagines the sound as a band of colour, turquoise whistling through rocky peaks. She harmonizes to the next oo, spins around, the tip of her nose against the cold tiled wall, so the next line is right in front of her, like lips against her ear, like someone else's breath. She sings on the vowels, and each overtone climbs higher, red, orange, yellow, green, blue, indigo, up, up, up ...

Then the singing stops. She can hear Matty shout, "Unplug it! Unplug it!" Then what must be Samantha's voice, "Oh my God!"

As Jane opens the bathroom door, water rushes to her feet like the tide coming in. The bar is already covered in an inch of water, but it is rising quickly. Richard is stuffing the napkin scraps into his coat pockets. Some drop to the water and he bends over to pinch them out. Aaron and Samantha are standing on the leather chairs now, her high heels sharp enough to poke a hole, and Ned is on the phone, saying, "We're flooding!" More water streams out from beneath the fire exit door, the force of this stream hinting at the mass of water behind it.

Aaron steps off the chair, knee deep now in water, and wades toward the door, takes the handle. Matty strides toward him, but before she can reach him, the door is open and water floods in.

Ilsa, now waist deep, glides toward the stairs that lead up to the street, but it is impossible to climb them. They are waterfalls now, rushing faster and faster.

The water rises to the phone. The stool seats bob along the surface like shiny black lily pads, held up by the foam sealed in vinyl. Jane treads water beside them, heavy in her boots. She takes a breath and lets herself sink below as she unties her boots. When she comes up again, her head is near the ceiling. Matty is holding onto a MacTac pillar. Ilsa is standing on the bar so her head is just above water, while Richard, Samantha, Aaron and Ned tread water in the cluttered sea, navigating through the stools, straws, half-empty jugs of liqueurs and grenadine to find something to hold onto.

The water rises. Matty is wide-eyed and speechless. When Jane sees this, she feels afraid. You don't look like that, she wants to say. The water rises past Matty's mouth. She points her nose to the ceiling and the water rises over her ears, to her eyes, to her nose.

And then they are all under water. Their chests are still, unable to take a breath, as they wait below, suspended. Ilsa's hair lifts off her head and floats up like a jellyfish. Richard's coat fans out at each side like a ray. For the moment, for this one still, breathless, moment, they are creatures of the sea. The mirror ball continues to spin, and the blue and red spotlights and neon signs continue to glow, so the light is tossed across Aaron's cheeks, flickering away from the cubic zirconia on Samantha's finger, splashing Matty's face, off the face of Ned's watch, like a spotlight flash to Richard, and raining back off Ilsa's green sequins, which Jane sees now could be so much more than sequins, more like a lost treasure or a mermaid's scales.

If Jane were not feeling so much fear and doubt, she might have enjoyed this moment, but instead, she feels sad because this must be her final destination. She begins to feel stabbing pain in her lungs as her body hiccups inside. She wants desperately to take a breath. Just as she feels she cannot control this reflex any longer—that she must inhale, saturate the blood with all the wrong elements—just as she is about to take the fatal breath, the feeling subsides. Her chest is still, full. It is as if she has only just taken a breath. Her skin tingles and she feels heat travel down her abdomen, wrap around her lower back, the backs of her thighs, the bottoms of her feet, as if every cell has swelled with oxygen. Seconds pass, but the feeling remains. She exhales through narrow lips, causing floating bits of napkin to swirl away. She is still full of breath. She exhales a little again. She has so much more! She looks at Matty, who is smiling now, floating toward Ilsa, who is also smiling, and taking her hand. Richard takes the rest of the napkins from his pockets and releases them. They swirl around him, lit up by the blue and red flickering lights.

Jane wants to call to him, but she imagines she will hear only the garbled sound of bubbles under water. She calls to him anyway, "You look like you're in a snow globe!"

The words are clear, warm and rounded, and she feels them vibrate through the water and tickle her skin.

Matty tries too, singing, "Woo-hoo!"

Richard howls like a wolf, while Aaron continues his improvisations to "oo." Then they are all singing and Jane can feel every vowel's vibration.

She closes her eyes, feels the oxygen charge her every cell, every cell charge the water molecules around her, which move outward, everywhere, and she sings, "Aaaah! Ooooh! Oooo! Eeee!" with all the others, the overtones ringing through the ocean, making shapes with Richard's snowflakes, and glittering off Ilsa's sequins. Jane is beside herself, watching her body sing, and flying through the water, soaring between stools and tables and playful dancers. She could swim up the stairs—they all could, maybe—up to the sidewalk. She could surface, she could. But it was all right here for now.

Andrea Routley's work has appeared in numerous literary magazines, including *The Malahat Review* and *Room Magazine*, and in 2008, she was shortlisted for the Rona Murray Prize for Literature. She is the founder and editor of *Plenitude Magazine*, Canada's queer literary magazine. She edited *Walk Myself Home: An Anthology to End Violence Against Women* (Caitlin Press, 2010), which continues to receive praise from magazines like *Bitch, Herizons, Prairie Fire* and the *Vancouver Sun*. In 2012, she completed a degree in writing from the University of Victoria. She currently lives in Victoria, BC, with her girlfriend and their ferocious cat, Travis.

Cover artist **Sandy Tweed** spent a decade teaching high school science followed by another as a building contractor. A new decade called for a new career. Having dabbled in watercolours in the past Sandy picked up her brushes and began painting again only to find herself uninspired. Looking to recapture the passion in her art she tried acrylic paints and found a bold and dynamic medium that suited her perfectly. The subjects of her paintings are no surprise given her childhood fascination for any and all critters and a bachelor of science degree in zoology.

Of the cover image Sandy says, "When focusing up close on nature I am sucked into the subject and all that exists is the connection between us. I hoped 'The Watcher' would share the depth of that connection, as well as raising the questions of what they might see when gazing back at us."

Sandy currently lives on the Oregon coast with her two dogs, Shaya and Luna. More of her work can be seen at www. sandytweed.com.